SPLASH

a novel by

M.E. RHINES

SPLASH

Copyright ©2019 M.E. Rhines
All rights reserved.
Printed in the United States of America
First Edition: February 2019

Clean Teen Publishing
WWW.CLEANTEENPUBLISHING.COM

Summary: Fawna is happy with the life she's made for herself on land. She has her child and her youngest sister Pauline by her side—plus an amazing new human boyfriend named Randy. So when an old friend from her underwater kingdom shows up, she immediately feels the weight of everything she stands to lose. But they bring news she can't ignore—Atargatis is in peril, and only she can help...

ISBN: 978-1-63422-314-0 (paperback)
ISBN: 978-1-63422-315-7 (e-book)
Cover Design by: Marya Heidel
Typography by: Courtney Knight
Editing by: Kelly Risser

COVER ART
©FOTOLIA/TVERDOHLIB
©FOTOLIA/YELLOWJ

Young Adult Fiction / Mermaids
Young Adult Fiction / Fairy Tales & Folklore / Adaptations
Young Adult Fiction / Legends, Myths, Fables / General

For more information about our content disclosure, please utilize the QR code above with your smart phone or visit us at
www.CleanTeenPublishing.com

FOR ALL WONDERFUL FANS OF ATARGATIS
AND ITS PRINCESSES.

CHAPTER 1

She was furious, that much was certain. With a violent rage, the ocean lobbed her waves at me, churning and toiling the polluted sands of the beach until the ground disintegrated from under my toes. I stumbled, catching myself just before the surf sucked me in, along with the submerging earth.

Forceful wind whipped at my neck, as if pushing me forward and edging me back home. The amulet dangling at my chest glinted in the moonlight, shining a beacon into the water. I lifted a trembling finger and peeled a salt-soaked strand of white hair from my cheek.

"What has you screaming so?" I whispered to the bits of froth and tiny whirlpools around me. In all the years I lived in the ocean, never once could I recall her so angry. Even when Pauline and I defied nature, plucking ourselves from the water's cocoon and choosing the land over her, she never struck with such venom.

I withdrew from the stinging whitecaps, seeking the safe haven of dry land. Staying in the water, even to my knees, wasn't safe. She would have me, if given the chance, and my sister would be left to wonder my fate.

We would send for Angelique, I decided. One of the porpoises in the area would fetch her if we asked. Our only ocean-bound sister would explain, even if she was still cross. It was her duty to report our kingdom's happenings, and I trusted she wouldn't falter in that responsibility.

In the meantime, I had my own pressing issues at hand. Decisions were to be made, and wondering at the mighty waves wouldn't make them go away.

Heading up the beach, I followed the pathway to our back porch with sluggish steps. Flashes of lights shone through the windows, slicing through the darkness and sending rocks to the pit of my stomach. The television was on, which meant Pauline was awake and waiting. As soon as I cracked the sliding glass door she would see my soiled clothes and start asking questions.

I was supposed to be on a date, not going for a swim.

By the time I creaked open the screen door and began dusting the sand from my bare feet, the living room lights flipped on. I groaned, pressing the heels of my palms against my eyes.

Sparkling violet eyes welcomed me as I stepped inside, and Pauline's sly smile spread across her face. "So, was I right? Did he ask you?"

She gleamed at me, expecting an answer, but my blasted human knees wobbled. Overcome with woozy weakness, I leaned back, resting my weight against the glass. Heat splashed across my cheeks, eliciting beads of sweat to pepper my brow.

"Fawna." Pauline gasped, reaching out for me.

"Are you all right? You're soaked."

A simple shake of the head was the most I could manage. Using her remarkable strength, my sister wedged herself under my arm and helped me hobble toward the sofa. Once I was seated, she grabbed a glass of water from the coffee table and thrust it into my shaking hand.

"Here. Take a drink and a breath. What's going on? Why are you all wet?"

The cool liquid saturated the scorching heat in my throat, banishing my panic into submission. For the moment, at least. When I was sure I could stomach the words, I uttered, "He asked me."

Her face brightened once more, the wide smile returning. "That's wonderful!"

"I'm not so sure it is, Pauline. I told him I had to think about it."

"You have to think about it? Randy is perfect for you. He makes you so happy, doesn't he?"

"Of course he does."

"He's always so kind to you."

"I know."

"Doting over your comfort, making sure you're pleased, he treats you like a princess, even without knowing you are one."

"Yes, yes." I tilted my head back, resting the back of my hand over my forehead. "All that and more. Randy is my perfect catch."

"He adores you. Sebastian, too."

At the statement, I swallowed hard. He didn't just adore me and my baby, he loved us, true and pure. I saw it in his eyes every time he beheld mine.

But then, the longer I gazed into his eyes, the sooner the smoky grey haze would morph into the soft green of Gene's, reminding me of what I had lost.

Of what I had done.

Randy was my opportunity at a second chance. I should be thrilled, but my heart was still too broken to bask in the blessing of it. In truth, I wasn't certain I deserved such happiness.

My guilt, however, was not something I would burden my youngest sister with.

I gestured toward my knees and chuckled. "There are a few things he should know before we marry, is there not? He's already started to question why I won't remove this bulky necklace."

"So you tell him."

"Pauline, you know as well as I do that it isn't that simple."

"If he loves you, he'll accept you for all of you."

"I'm not sure it's fair to expect him to just accept the fact that the woman he's been dating for the last year is half-fish."

Her cheeks splotched pink, and she pressed her lips into a hard line. "You're a mermaid, not a fish, and yes, it is fair. Eddie loves me despite our... differences."

"Eddie was unfortunate enough to find himself transplanted into our world. Mother forced him to witness the beauty along with the chaos."

"Well, not exactly. I was the one who kissed him. It was my fault, but I won't apologize for it. It brought us together."

Patting her hand with my own, I smiled. "I'm

pleased it worked out for you. My situation, however, is much different."

"Do you love him?"

"Of course I love him."

"Then I don't see a difference."

"This isn't about love, it's about logic. Randy has no inkling mermaids even exist. He'd think I was insane if I told him what we are."

"Oh please." Pauline made a show of rolling her eyes and sputtering her lips. "He works on a commercial fishing boat, Fawna. I'm sure he's come across plenty of things on the open ocean that pointed toward our existence."

I nibbled my lip, pondering the idea. "Maybe."

"Besides, if he doesn't believe you, you could always take off that medallion and show him."

"Right," I said with a chuckle. "Could you imagine his face as I shifted before his horrified eyes? He'd run away screaming, without a doubt."

"There's nothing horrifying about your tail," she chastised, poking my ribs with a bony finger. "Have a little faith, Fawna. If there's one thing I know for certain, it's that love always prevails."

I let loose a quaking sigh, observing my sister's innocent view of the world with a fierce jealousy. Wisdom could be found within its simplicity, I couldn't deny as much. But, fear still weaved itself tight around my heart, threatening to squeeze out any lasting droplets of hope.

There was no way in the ocean I could tell Randy what I was. If he rejected me, saw me as a monster or some unlovable thing... It would break me. I couldn't rebound from such heartbreak twice.

There would be no explaining this to such an impossible romantic, however. Lifting my cheeks into a pretend smile, I nodded. "I believe I'm the older sister, am I not? You shouldn't be the one doling out such brilliant insight on cue."

Ever pleased with the compliment, a twinkle found her violet eyes as she leaned in to embrace me. "You forget I've seen much more in my years as a merling than most humans do in a lifetime. I've learned a thing or two."

"So, we're all grown up, then. If mother could see you now." A rap at the door pulled me to my feet. I ruffled her jet-black hair as I passed, making a mess of the already frizzy strands. She shrieked playfully, pulling away and swatting at me before following in my steps.

"Who could it be this late?" she asked. "Probably Randy. I bet he misses you already."

Unlocking the deadbolt, I groaned. "It's not Randy. He's taking the boat out before sunrise, so he should be in bed by now."

Pauline pushed out her lips, taunting me with kisses to the air. "He just couldn't stay away."

"Oh, that's quite enough of that." I swung the door open, jumping back at the flash of radiant blue hair quivering on my front steps. My lips tingled as the blood rushed from my face and I announced, "Jewel? What are you—"

"Wait, what?" Pauline shoved me aside, but I peered over her short stature with ease.

Jewel, my younger sister's best friend in the sea,

trembled before us. Dripping wet and completely naked, she wrapped her arms around her breasts to cover herself. Her teeth chattered, the sound mingling with that of clanking metal. A medallion, matching the ones Pauline and I both wore, tangled at the base of her throat.

Mouth agape, my gaze lingered over the girl's milky-white knee caps. Stunned for the second time this evening, I blinked, wishing away what had to be a hallucination. This couldn't be my sister's spirited and spunky side kick.

She had no tail.

The color drained from Pauline's cheeks as she took in the sight, but Jewel merely lifted an eyebrow and scolded, "What, the human world took your manners along with your fins? It's freezing out here!"

Remembering myself, I seized the feisty mermaid by her arm and yanked her inside, out of view. "Good Poseidon," I mumbled. "Pauline, fetch her a towel and some of your clothes."

Scrambling to do as I asked, Pauline disappeared into her bedroom before emerging again, holding the towel out for the taking. I snatched it from her grasp, then wrapped it around the shivering mess of a now-human.

"Jewel..." Pauline stared, dumbfounded. "What... what on earth are you doing here?"

"It can wait until she's dressed," I insisted. "The bathroom is right down the hall."

"The what?"

"A small room with running water. Just go in, put these clothes on and then we can talk."

"But this is an urgent matter! Who cares if my human parts are showing?"

I snickered a little, shaking my head. Mermaids weren't exactly modest creatures. It was a trait I picked up living amongst the humans. "It's for your own good. You'll warm up if you've got something covering you. It's right in there."

Huffing, the mermaid followed my pointed finger, and moments later, reemerged clothed. Her eyes zeroed in on me, a desperate panic gleaming in her irises.

"Now," I said to her, "what has brought you so far from home?"

"I had to warn you. She's coming for Sebastian."

Pauline's strangled gasp barely registered as the girl's words sucked the air from my lungs, replacing the oxygen with a suffocating emptiness that constricted my throat. Shock gave way to a maternal rage, and my fists curled involuntarily at my side.

She was talking about my baby.

"Who?" I barked, aware and uncaring that my cool was all but gone.

"I'm not sure," she answered.

"Is it Mother? Because I swear to Poseidon— "

Jewel clutched at her towel with one hand and waved the other in the air in a furiously quick motion. "No, no. Queen Calypso isn't the culprit, though she has gone missing."

"If she's gone missing, then how do you know it isn't her?"

"Because whoever came hunting for the heir *took* your mother."

"You're not making any sense," Pauline protested.

Jewel turned to my sister, but I gathered her shoulders in my grip and twisted her back to me. "What's going on, Jewel? What's happened?"

"It's chaos." The girl took in a shaky breath. "Someone... a nemesis of your mother's, stormed the kingdom. They ransacked the palace, took nearly all of our people prisoner, including Queen Calypso. I, myself, only just escaped."

Pauline squeaked, then covered her quivering lips with her palm. My own stomach roiled, a sickening nausea sweeping over me. Guilt chiseled painful cracks into my heart, attacking with such force I grabbed at my chest. I should've been there. Whatever plight my people fought, I should have been right beside them.

"What of my Aunt Myrtle?" I asked. "Is she captive as well? Tell me she was able to flee with you."

Jewel's mouth turned downward, and her spine stiffened at my inquiry. Her sullen face answered even before the words left her lips. "Queen Myrtle fought the trespasser until her very last breath."

CHAPTER
2

Pauline's frantic sobs filled the room, forcing me to remain stoic and composed for the both of us. As much as my knees wanted to buckle, I couldn't allow it. Collapsing would prevent me from being my sister's pillar. I collected her slender fingers with my own, offering her some stability in my hold.

"And... our sister," I started, hesitant. I wasn't sure I could bear hearing I had lost her as well. "What has become of Angelique?"

"She remains in the Orkney Islands with the fin-folk. I doubt she even knows of the attack yet."

I squinted at her. "The Orkney Islands," I echoed. "What in Poseidon's name is she doing so far north?"

"Haven't you heard? Surely your sister informed you of her engagement to the fin-man."

Pauline clenched my knuckles between her own. I winced at the pain from her tightening clasp, but through her shock, she didn't notice. "She's... she's marrying one of the fin-men?" she asked, disbelief saturating her words. "One of the barbarians that tried to overtake our kingdom?"

"Lennox," Jewel stated with a flat nod. "He didn't fight with his people, though. He was on our side.

I'm surprised Angelique hasn't told you all about him. He's all she cares to speak of to anyone."

A lump of resentment lodged itself in my throat. I shook my head, a feeble attempt at banishing the feeling, and responded, "No. We've spoken very little since she brought Sebastian to us. We only learned of the conflict between the clans through a messenger dispatched by our sister."

"Consider yourselves lucky you didn't have to see it firsthand. It was a dreadful and violent attack. The kingdom only just survived."

"We should've been there," I confessed, ashamed. "Two more spears could've made a lot of difference."

"I don't think it would've made much of an impact." She shrugged. "There were a lot of really big warriors on their side, mostly male. Besides, we won. That's what counts."

"Even if we could've saved one life..."

"I've seen Pauline with a dagger," she teased, tossing my sister a wink. "Trust me, she wouldn't have done much good."

Pauline stared ahead, pale and unflinching, as if she hadn't even heard the jab. Jewel snapped her fingertips an inch away from Pauline's eyes to gain her attention. "Hello! Earth to Pauline."

"Are you all right?" I asked.

She scrunched her nose up and shivered. "A fin-man? My sister is marrying a fin-man?"

Jewel rolled her eyes. "Hey, they're not all monsters. I met a pretty nice one myself, actually."

"You what?"

"I'm not about to move to the northern waters

for him or anything. It's not *that* serious. Then again, I might consider it if it meant I could be queen, like Angelique. She and Lennox are going to be the new rulers of Finfolkaheem. Good Poseidon, that mermaid leads an exciting life. Queen no matter where she goes."

I arched a brow. "She's taking the throne of another kingdom even after the demise of Queen Myrtle?"

"Well she..." Jewel's voice grew quiet, her eyes shifting to the ground. "As I mentioned, she doesn't know. I'm certain she will return once she hears, but I had to warn you before I went to find Angelique."

"You said someone — something is after Sebastian," I recalled, glancing toward the closed door to the nursery. My heavy chest filled with a sudden urge to burst in his room and gather him up. "What makes you so certain that you would rush here so quick you wouldn't even think to clothe yourself first?"

"After the attack, I went searching for survivors. The queen was barely breathing when I found her, but she managed to hang on just long enough to give me this." She lifted the amulet. "Queen Myrtle said to find you at once. To warn you that the sea witch that took your mother won't stop until she has him."

"But why?" Pauline protested. "We've left the ocean and taken him with us. We're no threat to this witch!"

"He's the first male born to the royal family for centuries. At least, the first surviving one. There's great potential flowing through his veins. I imagine in the right hands, the magic lacing his blood could be very powerful. And from what I saw, this... thing would know exactly what to do with it."

"She wants to kill him," I said, numbly.

Jewel was quick to reject the notion. "No, Fawna, we don't know that. She could have a way to extract his essence without killing him."

My sister's eyes grew wide, and she reached to me for guidance. "What should we do?"

Overwhelmed, I sank down onto the sofa, pressing the heels of my palms against my eyes. Instinct told me to stay put; to keep Sebastian and my sister as far away from the ocean as possible. We could move further inland, maybe to the mountains, even. Logic, however, revealed how naïve the notion was.

Magic was a skill I wielded myself, quite well, actually. But, Myrtle was the most powerful sea witch I'd ever known, in many ways even more gifted than Mother, and still this new threat defeated her. Not only that, but she managed to pluck the terrible Queen Calypso from her cell and carry her off like a common prisoner. Clearly, we were outmatched. If my aunt possessed the power to transform our bodies and transfer us to land, no doubt the enemy could, too.

It didn't matter where we were. As long as this evil breathed, none of us were safe.

What I wouldn't give to rewind twenty minutes. To go back to when my most troublesome decision was whether or not I wanted to spend the rest of my life with a captain and his boat. They came as a pair, I'd learned. To love one meant to accept the other.

How could I marry him knowing at any given moment a leisurely outing could become a catastrophic disaster? The darkness lurking beneath the waves would swallow him up in an instant, all just to get to me and my baby.

"Fawna." Pauline's whimper beckoned me from the darkness. "Atargatis is without a ruler."

"Angelique was bequeathed the throne," I pointed out.

Jewel shook her head, her blue hair still sprinkling little droplets of water. "When her engagement was announced, Queen Myrtle amended it. As it stands, you're the acting queen of Atargatis."

A sweltering heat latched onto the back of my neck, making me dizzy. "I'm what?"

"Yeah." A small smirk started in the corner of her mouth. "So, should I bow or something?"

I opened my mouth to retort, but a jolting thud came from the other side of Sebastian's door. The hair on my arms stood on end as the unmistakable clatter of shattering glass jerked me to my feet. I leapt up, darting across the room and shoving my way past Jewel and Pauline.

Sheer panic surged through me as I barreled into the door with my shoulder, but the knob was stuck and the barrier unyielding. "It won't open," I shrieked.

"Here, let me." Pauline nudged me out of the way, lifted a foot and hammered the wooden surface again and again until it splintered and crashed to the ground. Once again, I gawked at her tremendous strength, taking just a moment to thank Poseidon for blessing her with it before rushing past her.

From the broken window, an unnatural wind gushed into the room, fighting against my every step. A torrent of unbridled magic saturated the air, zapping my skin with little blue sparks of electricity. The farther I stepped into the room, the more the shocks intensified, electrocuting me. My knees threatened to buckle, more and more, every inch closer to Sebastian's cradle. Determined, I pressed through the burns. Nothing would keep me from getting to him. *Nothing.*

The bed's frame scalded my skin as I collided with the crib, the wood burning hot and smoking. I couldn't be bothered to flinch. My attention was drawn to the cold, empty spot in the center of the mattress where Sebastian should be sleeping.

"No," I whispered, flattening my palms against the sheet before bunching them together to make fists. "No!"

Tendrils of smoke drifted down from the ceiling. The black smog slithered as if alive, twisting itself down and around. I watched it descend, mesmerized until I realized it was wrapping itself around Pauline's neck. Her eyes bulged, and she clutched at her throat as the black magic tightened its grip.

Jewel stood frozen in the doorway, in a trance. The whites of her eyes glazed over her irises, striking me with a fear that made my whole body go numb. It was Jewel's small frame in front of me, but the person looking through her eyes was not a member of my clan.

"Stop this," I screamed at Jewel's possessor as I

lunged for my sister. She didn't. Instead, she tilted her head to the side, as if analyzing the swollen veins in Pauline's neck, trying to figure out how to draw out the suffering without making it pop entirely.

My touch passed through the smoke that strangled Pauline, whose desperate eyes scanned the room for any help at all. A seething rage burned in my core as I watched her struggle. This thing had already taken my baby; it wouldn't have my sister, as well.

I turned my attention back to Jewel. If I couldn't disperse the magic, I would have to take down the witch creating it. Winding back, I slapped her hard across the face, gathered her arms up and shook her like a piece of seaweed. "Come back, damn it! Jewel, you're killing her."

The whites of her eyes cooked black, the bridge of her nose turning ashen and haunted. A wicked smile crossed her lips, and she spoke in a raspy, echoing voice that boomed against my eardrums with painful force. "Search for us and you will see how evil I can truly be. Let the merman serve his purpose, and I will let your sister live. Come after him, and I will have her head."

"What... who are you?"

The coal color polluting Jewel's eyes simmered away, leaving behind their natural bright blue. A blinding bolt of lightning struck Sebastian's crib. I brought my arm up to cover my eyes, and when I dropped it down again, both my sister and her friend laid in crumpled heaps on the floor, unconscious.

Rushing to her side, I fell next to Pauline, throwing myself on top of her. Her chest rose rapidly, a strange slick, flapping noise keeping in rhythm with her breath. The smothering smoke had evaporated, but her lips still held a twinge of blue and her lungs gurgled.

I held her face, tilting her head back to check her throat for an obstruction of some sort. The ice-cold metal of her medallion cooled the burns on my forearm as it brushed my skin, and that's when I noticed it. The original golden shine was faded to rust, calcified with green mineral. Examining it closer, I pulled the chain taut, the movement itself causing the necklace to disintegrate into dust. There, under a thick layer of bruising and burst capillaries, I found the source of the alien sound.

Blemishing the milky white skin on each side of her neck were gill slits. Stunned, I toppled backward. She was drowning. The realization was enough to force me to my feet. Unlike my sister, I wasn't particularly sturdy, but I took hold of her ankles and managed to drag her to the bathroom. There, I rolled her up and over the lip of the tub, shuddering as she landed with a thump. I plugged up the drain and turned on the water before hurrying back to Sebastian's room.

The fresh water would keep her alive for a short while, but I had to get her to the ocean.

"Wake up!" I crouched over Jewel's lifeless body, shaking her. "Jewel, please, wake up!"

My heart skipped a beat when she groaned a bit, and when her eyes fluttered open I could've fainted. "Thank Poseidon," I murmured.

She coughed, hacking out puffs of grey soot. The remnants left behind by the being who forced her way in Jewel's body. Her eyes watered, and when she finally sucked in enough clean air, she caught her breath.

"Why do my insides feel like they're on fire?" she wondered aloud.

"The witch used you as a conduit."

Her face brightened pink as she ran her hands along her chest. "She was in my body? That's disgusting! What does she want?"

"We were too late. She took Sebastian."

"I remember that. I'm sorry, Fawna. We'll find him."

"She said if we go looking for him... she'll kill Pauline in an act of retribution."

Jewel launched forward, her still new legs stumbling under her body. "If that witch lays one drop of magic on her I swear I'll—"

"She already has."

"What?" She looked around the room, suddenly aware that Pauline wasn't in it. "Where's Pauline?" Before I could answer, she followed the sound of running water to the bathroom, her scream piercing another hole in what little self-control I had left.

CHAPTER 3

Behind the safe haven of his dark sunglasses, I couldn't see his eyes. I didn't need to. They didn't protect either of us from the pain they masked. Randy rubbed at his chin, playing with his sandy whiskers as if their familiarity brought him comfort.

He leaned back; the café table between us was too small a barrier. Behind him, the ocean's waves rolled onto the shoreline. Any other time, this deck was our special place. Our favorite restaurant with the perfect romantic scenery.

This time, though, instead of thinking of how perfect my view was with him and beach to stare at, my thoughts were focused on my sister. Trapped in the ocean, waiting for me to join her. At least she had Jewel, I reminded myself. The two were inseparable now that Pauline was back in the water.

A few threads of his salted blond hair danced in the breeze, and I followed them, welcoming the distraction. The firm set of his angular jaw tensed, the muscle in his forearm flexing as he tapped his index finger against the bristles.

Don't cry, I commanded myself. It would do neither of us any good.

"Just tell me one thing," he summoned, his voice low. "Is it another man?"

My jaw fell open. "Of course not! How could you think such a thing?"

"Then what's this all about, Fawna? Because I could swear just a couple days ago we were happy. Now, not only are you saying you can't marry me, but you're skipping town to boot."

"I know it seems odd—"

"Odd? Hell, I'm used to odd as far as you're concerned. Everything about you is so damn odd. The way you look at the world around you with such awe, like it's your first time experiencing every little thing. How you spend hours alone in the ocean just talking to dolphins like they can understand every word you say. Or how if anybody even touches that necklace around your neck you have a panic attack. You are odd, and I love it. I love every quirk that you have. But this, this is... heartless."

"I'm not doing this to hurt you, Randy."

"Then why are you doing it?"

I dropped my gaze to the ground. "I can't tell you that."

"Listen." He propped his elbows on the table, leaning closer. "I don't want to sound like a jerk here, but I think you owe me better than that. I'm not just losing you, remember that. That little boy means the world to me, Fawna."

He was right. In all the time we'd been together, he had treated me with nothing but the utmost patience and respect. Sebastian, as far as he was concerned, was his own flesh and blood. He loved us both, and we loved him just as much. Randy deserved an explanation, and I wished with all my heart I could give him the truth.

"Something's happened," I explained. "With my family, I mean. I have to go home for a while, maybe for good."

"All right, that's a start. Maybe if you tell me what's going on I can help."

"That's sweet of you, Randy, but it wouldn't be safe to involve you in it."

He slid his glasses down, letting them dangle on their cord around his neck. "Are you saying you're in some kind of danger? Because if you are, you don't have to face it by yourself. I want to be there for you, for your family. Pauline's like a sister to me, too, you know?"

"I know she is, and I know you want to help but... you can't."

"What's she got to say about all this? She can't be happy about just picking up and taking off. Her boyfriend is here, her friends are here. You're taking her away from her life and everyone she loves."

"Pauline has already left. She understands this is what we have to do."

Randy's face fell, more hurt pulling at his features. "She didn't even say goodbye."

"She wanted to," I insisted. "This wasn't exactly planned, Randy, believe me. Pauline had to go right away, without saying goodbye to anyone."

"It's about your mother, isn't it? Eddie told me she's been in prison."

I tensed, immediately put on edge. My sister's

boyfriend should know better than to speak about such things. Our family matters were kept secret for a reason. Any hint at our origins could put my entire clan in jeopardy.

"Eddie has a big mouth," I grumbled. "And I'll be sure to tell him so the next time he's unfortunate enough to run into me."

"Don't go getting mad at him. If you and Pauline weren't secretive about everything he wouldn't have to cover for you. What I can't understand is, if Pauline trusts Eddie enough to tell him your secrets, why can't you trust me?"

I rubbed my eyes, willing back a mounting headache. The onslaught of questions chipped away at my patience, my lack of sleep fueling my temper. Taking in a calming breath, I steadied myself. None of this was Randy's fault.

"It isn't as simple as you make it sound."

"I think it is."

"That's because you don't know anything!" I shouted, slamming a fist down on the table.

Randy shrank back at my outburst, no doubt just as humiliated as I was at the sudden attention of the surrounding patrons. "I'm sorry," I whispered, guilt hitting my stomach.

"Maybe I don't know anything," he said, his voice trembling, "but just remember that's only because you refuse to fill me in."

He stood up, the legs of his chair scraping against the wooden deck.

"Randy, wait," I begged, but he stormed off, ignoring my plea. I reached into my purse, pulled out a wad of cash without counting the bills and tossed them on the table before taking off after him.

In the parking lot, to my surprise, he leaned against his car, waiting with arms folded in front of his chest. I approached slowly, afraid any sudden movement might frighten him away for good. Once I was within arms-length, he snaked his arm around my torso and yanked me against him until our bodies molded together.

My instincts to pull away were useless; when he held me this way, I couldn't resist resting my forehead against his, breathing in his closeness until his scent filled my lungs. Atargatis, the Keys, it didn't matter where I went. If Randy wasn't with me, it could never be home.

Without thinking, I shifted my weight to my toes and lifted myself up, closing the distance between our mouths. A familiar flame sparked in my heart, the same intoxicating warmth that always accompanied his kiss. Every time our lips met, the fire burned anew. His fingers found their natural place at the nape of my neck, tangling in the silk of my white hair. My chest ached, as if my soul recognized this would be the last time my heart would ever feel this close to whole ever again.

"You can't leave me," he choked out, pulling back just enough to look into my eyes. "You're everything to me, Fawna. You can't go."

"I don't have a choice," I squeaked, afraid if I said anything more I would fall to pieces.

"Then let me come with you. I'll follow you anywhere. We'll get in my boat and just go."

"Where I'm going you can't follow. You or your precious boat," I teased.

"You make it sound like you're going to Venus. That's the big secret, isn't it? You're an alien. That's why you're such an odd swan."

I chuckled. "I think the expression is an odd duck."

"You're much too beautiful to be compared to a waddling duck. With that white hair and those big silver eyes, you could pass for a swan in disguise."

"You say the strangest things."

"Haven't you ever seen the Swan Princess?"

"No," I giggled, shaking my head.

"It's about a girl who turns into a swan, like a werewolf except... a swan."

"You humans and your fairytales."

He pointed an accusing finger at me, "There, see? You always say that. 'You humans', like you're not one of us. Tell me the truth: are you a swan or an alien?"

"If I admitted to either you'd have me thrown in a hospital before I could skip town. I'm on to your nefarious plans. Nice try!"

"Nah. I don't think either of those things is so far out there." Randy released me, then shoved his hand through his hair. "I've seen some things out on the open sea you wouldn't believe."

I cocked my head at him, reading into his words. It wasn't unheard of for a mermaid to have a run-in with fishermen. Spending as much time as he did out on the boat, it could be possible...

"Tell me about them."

He rubbed his neck, a shy presence befalling him. "No way. You'd be the one throwing me in the looney bin."

"Try me. Come on now, I'm curious."

"Swear you won't laugh."

I made an X over my chest with my index finger. "Cross my heart. No laughter."

He looked around, making sure the coast was clear before starting his story. "A while back, when Reggie captained the ship, we were trawling way out in the triangle."

My throat went dry at mention of the landmark. If he meant what I thought he did, it put him right in Atargatis's waters. I cleared my voice, then asked, "The Bermuda Triangle, you mean?"

"That's right," he confirmed with a short bob of the head. "The net got caught on something heavy, and this is where it gets weird, I swear to God we pulled a mermaid out of the water. At first I thought it was just a girl lost at sea, but she had the most beautiful blue tail."

CHAPTER
4

My face went numb, and I fought to maintain an emotionless expression. "A mermaid," I repeated. "Are you... are you sure about that? Maybe you were out at sea just a bit too long. The sun can play tricks on the mind, you know."

"I know, I know. It sounds nuts, but it's true, I swear it. And it gets even more bizarre."

"You have no idea," I mumbled, unintentionally.

"What's that?"

"Nothing. Go on. I'm listening, no judgement I swear."

"When we captured her, the sea changed. It was like the water came alive. Waves drove into our boat like the ocean was desperate to have her back. A whirlpool came out of nowhere, and just before it sucked us in, the rigging broke, releasing the net she was in. She got back to the water; I just wish I knew if she made it out alive."

I smiled to myself, biting my lip and averting my gaze. Whatever mermaid they took from the sea, she must've been dreadfully important for the sea to intervene. The sea preferred to stay out of the affairs of humans, keeping her position neutral on most fronts. Though on the rare occasion, she had been known to take sides with devastating force.

Considering his revelation ignited a tiny ember of hope. He believed in my kind, had even seen one of my clan members. I still had to leave, my responsibilities left me with no choice in that. Maybe, though, I didn't have to abandon Randy without explanation. Perhaps if I could tell him the truth, the whole truth, it would soften the blow, if even just a little.

Convincing him of what I was would be the easy part. The possibility that he would tell anyone, however, still posed a great danger for my clan. Could I trust him? He was a decent man, kind and honest, but fear could make humans act in ways they wouldn't under normal circumstances.

"You think I'm crazy," he said, blushing bright pink.

"No, no. I'm just wondering... were you frightened?"

"I don't think 'frightened' is the right word. Actually, she fascinated me. Even outside her element, suspended high in the air above her home, there was something graceful and enchanting about her. I don't know, maybe it was just because she was a living fairytale brought to life right in front of my face, but I couldn't take my eyes off her."

"I'm sure it was an experience you'll cherish always."

"A mermaid. A real mermaid caught in my net. I wouldn't have believed my own eyes if Reggie hadn't seen her, too."

"I'm sure the two of you were eager to tell the tale to your seafaring comrades," I hinted, testing the waters. "No pun intended."

"Reggie was. As soon as we got to shore he ran his mouth to anyone who would listen."

"What about you?"

"No, you're the first person I've ever told. Partly because of the way people reacted when Reggie went on about it. They thought he had lost his mind. He hasn't been able to nab a fishing gig since, that's how I got his position as captain."

"And... the other reason?"

Randy fidgeted a bit before stuffing his hands in his pockets and looking away. "I don't know, I guess I feel like she deserves to be left alone. Could you imagine what people would do to her kind if they found out? They'd be hunted just for the sport of it. We'd have mermaid exhibits all over the place and scientists dissecting them. She was intelligent; I could see it in her eyes. Mermaids should be left where they are if you ask me."

That was enough, the perfect response that told me everything I needed to know. Taking his hand, I pulled him away from his car, heading toward the beach. "Come with me."

"I thought you were in such a hurry to get out of here?"

"Right. And you're going to see me off properly."

He glanced ahead, toward the docks. "You're taking a boat?"

"No, no boat." I led him down the beach, kicking up sand and soaking in the gritty sensation between my toes. This could be the last time I would ever feel it, and I wanted to memorize how it felt. We walked under the boardwalk, just below where we had just been dining. Out of sight from tourists and hidden from the sun.

Randy stopped short, just as my legs felt the spray of the shoreline. "We're going for a swim? Now? I know how much you love the water, Fawna, but neither of us has our swimsuits."

I released his hand and turned toward him, backing slowly into the water. "I don't need it. You wanted to learn my deep dark secret, didn't you, Randy?"

"I figured it out, remember?" he teased. "You're from Venus. I can deal with an alien girlfriend."

Slipping a finger beneath the chain holding my amulet, I stared at him, watching close for a reaction. Something lurched inside my stomach, and I took a deep breath. "Are you sure you want to know? There's no going back once you see the truth."

"Of course I'm sure," he answered with conviction. "I need to know everything about you."

"Come closer." I backed deeper into the water until the waves crested at my midriff before I lifted my necklace up and over my head.

A familiar shock jolted me, accompanied with the uncomfortable tugging sensation as the skin on my legs fused together. My feet lifted from underneath me, twisting behind as they webbed together into a glistening silver fork. A prickling spread across the sides of my neck, and I sucked a breath in as my gills finished forming.

I dunked under the water, breathing in the first underwater breath I had taken in ages. The saltwater burned my eyes, though only for a moment before they readjusted. The jostling of the currents bobbed me up and down, back and forth like a cradle. The sea welcomed me in her embrace, wrapping her bubbles around me.

I was home.

My tongue danced along the edges of my mouth, raking up bits of salt and brine as they slid across my flesh. It wasn't until this moment that I realized how much I missed being the real me. Human life was exciting, full of adventure, but this tail... it was a part of me.

As I resurfaced, slowly and full of anxiety, I smacked my tail on the surface of the water, giving Randy the full view. The color drained from his cheeks, and he rubbed his eyes with his fists before blinking hard and taking another look at me.

I raised my arms above the water, a careful smile dancing across my lips. "Well. What do you think?"

He stumbled back, then rushed forward. Clothes and all, he dove into the water, swimming for me. "You're a mermaid," he announced now that he had me up close.

"I am. You're not scared?"

A twinkle flashed in his eye, and he reached out to stroke my cheek with the back of his fingers. "I didn't think it was possible, but you're even more beautiful with a tail."

"You're a liar," I accused with a giggle. "I'm a monster to your world."

He shook his head, hard and with purpose. "Not a monster, a fairytale. A stunning, magnificent fairytale."

"You're taking this a little too well," I remarked, narrowing my eyes at him. Perhaps he had been suspicious all along, waiting for me to come out with the truth.

"I'd probably be pretty freaked out if I hadn't already seen that girl. Actually, I'm relieved. I'm not gonna lie, deep down I thought maybe all those people who called Reggie nuts could be right, that the sea sickness got to us. Now I know it's true. You're real." He smiled, the creases of his eyes showing just how pleased he truly was at the sight of me. "You're really real."

"That I am."

"It all makes sense now. All your little quirks. That necklace has some kind of magic in it, right?"

"It does. My aunt is... was... a powerful sea witch. She created these so Pauline could follow Eddie, and I held a fascination for your world for as long as I can remember, so I joined them."

"Pauline and Eddie are mermaids, too?"

"Just Pauline. Eddie is completely human. It's a long story. The short version is they fell in love, and this was the only way they could be together."

"Something straight out of a Disney movie."

"The Little Mermaid," I said, rolling my eyes. "It was the first movie Eddie made us watch when we arrived on land."

"So, are there many of you? I know there's more out there, since Reggie and I caught one and all, but how many?"

"Enough. Our clan is small, but there are many others inhabiting the ocean. Different species of water folk, many of them very different than us."

He took the amulet from me, examining it closer. "Does it work in reverse? I mean, if I put it on will it turn me into a mermaid?"

"You mean a merman?" I chuckled. "No, I'm afraid it doesn't work like that."

"Man, that's a shame. I'd love to see your home."

"Perhaps one day you can," I offered, "but not as it stands. There's too much turmoil to bring you to my kingdom."

"Is that where you're going? Home?"

I nodded, dunked back under for a breath, and then explained, "My aunt only recently perished, killed by one of my mother's enemies. Now, Mother is missing, which means my kingdom, Atargatis, has no ruler to speak of and they're left in shambles."

"Your mother was in charge of your clan?"

"She was the queen. Now, I guess I am for the time being. The kingdom needs saving, and I get the job by default."

"Wow. That's pretty rough, Fawna. I'm sorry, I had no idea."

"There's no way you could have known."

"Wait, I thought Eddie said your mother was in prison?"

"She was. My aunt held her in a cell at the palace once she overthrew her. With good cause, mind you. The transition was welcomed, even by my sisters and me."

"She must've really done something awful to get thrown into the pen by her own sister with her own daughters signing the order."

My spine stiffened at the truth in his statement. Awful didn't begin to cover it, but I didn't care to go into the details of my mother's crimes. Not with Randy. I couldn't bear to have him look at me and wonder if that kind of evil lingered somewhere deep in my heart, waiting for a chance to escape. He could never know about Gene, and the terrible fate I allowed to befall him. Randy would never look at me the same.

"I'm afraid I haven't the time to rehash the story. It's a long and nightmare-inducing tale. Pauline's waiting for me in open waters, and we have to hurry."

"Will you at least tell me where you're going?"

"Home. In the center of the triangle, probably pretty close to where you caught that mermaid. I'm almost certain it was a member of my clan."

"If you find her... tell her I'm sorry. I almost let Reggie talk me into cashing her in. She looked like she understood every word of it. Don't want her thinking I'm... you know, a terrible person."

I gathered the collar of his shirt in my fists, pulling him close. "I'll be sure to sing your praises to her."

"Come back to me, Fawna. When you've settled everything, come home." He lowered his mouth over mine, trying to kiss me goodbye.

I jerked away, remembering what would happen if I kissed him without the medallion. He would grow gills the way Eddie had and become ocean bound. We could be together, rule Atargatis as King and Queen. As tempting as the thought seemed, I couldn't condemn him to it. He had a family here. Without Myrtle around to forge another magical necklace, there would be no return for him.

"Will you come back?" he asked again, swallowing hard at my perceived rejection.

As much as I wanted to appease him, to promise to return to the shore when all was said and done, I couldn't commit to it. There was a good chance I wasn't getting out of this conflict alive, and even if I did, there was a kingdom depending on me to put it back together. With Angelique occupied in her new territory, I couldn't shirk this responsibility. No matter how much I wanted to be with Randy.

"Goodbye, Randy," I said, my voice shaking. "I love you."

I turned, dashing under the water as quick as I could. Even through the thundering waves and quick current I heard him calling after me. Once there was a bit of distance between us, enough to keep him from reaching me, I surfaced and looked back at him.

He waved his arms over his head, yelling Sebastian's name. "Where's the baby?" he asked. "Should I look after him until you come back?"

My heart stopped beating, that pesky tightness in my throat returning. I couldn't lie to him, not about this. "She took him," I answered, thrashing my tail underneath me to keep up with the bouncing current. "The same witch who kidnapped my mother came for Sebastian."

Randy stood stunned, a fury building in his eyes. I half expected him to charge in the water, to believe himself capable of keeping up with me and embarking on this rescue by my side. Instead, he stomped toward the shoreline, circled around the boardwalk, and headed toward the docks, straight for his boat.

"Oh, Randy," I groaned to myself before descending again to search for Pauline and Jewel. We needed to get as far away from shore as possible. If he couldn't find us, he couldn't follow us into a potential slaughter.

CHAPTER 5

"Let's get moving." I raced toward Jewel and Pauline, who sat patiently waiting on a bed of coral offshore. My tail ached, already worn out from lack of practice. It had been so long since I enjoyed a good stretch of the fins, but now wasn't the time to sulk about how much I'd missed the feel of it.

Dashing past them, I ignored my sister when she called out for me to slow down. Randy's boat was fast, but I was faster, plus I had a head start. Only once we reached deeper waters where we could sink down into the depth, hidden from the surface and anyone on the other side of it, did I stop to catch my breath.

"For Poseidon's sake," Jewel complained through ragged huffs. "Didn't even take a minute to get your sea fins back, did you?"

"We don't have time to ease into things," I pointed out.

Pauline snatched my hand, bringing me to an abrupt stop mid-stroke. "Are you going to tell me what happened with Randy?"

"There's nothing to tell. He went his way and I went mine."

"You're lying." She pressed her lips into a hard line. "I hate when you lie to me."

Releasing a slow, steady breath, I acknowledged her complaint with a slow nod. It was a habit I had gotten myself into during Mother's reign. Surviving under Queen Calypso meant becoming a master of deceit, and by now I was an expert at the art. So much so, I could look my own sister in the eye and tell a lie without as much as a flinch.

"I'm sorry," I offered, ashamed. "I showed him what we are."

Jewel gasped, covering her mouth in shock. "You changed in front of a human?"

"Stop it," Pauline ordered her. "Randy wouldn't ever tell our secret. Most humans are nothing like the humans in Ms. Star's fish tales, including him. He's like Eddie. We can trust him."

"Well, I hope you're right about that."

"She is," I confirmed. "I took as long as I did to tell him because I had to be certain."

"Well?" Pauline prodded. "What did he say?"

"Actually, it was easier than I thought it'd be. He told me a story about him and Reggie catching a mermaid in their net, and I took the opportunity."

This time, Jewel squealed her distaste. "He caught a mermaid? You trusted a fisherman with a secret like this? Wow, Fawna. Bad call."

"It's not like he scooped her up and brought her ashore," I said, louder than intended. "No offense, Jewel, but you've never even met him so I'd appreciate it if you kept your second-hand knowledge of humans to yourself. Pauline and I have lived among them."

"Gone soft toward them, more like."

"Jewel!" Pauline shouted before I could. "May I remind you that you're speaking to the queen of Atargatis?"

The blue-haired mermaid shrank back, paling at her misstep, but I whipped my head from side to side, quick to call off the power-trip uttered on my behalf. "No, no, no. Don't play that card for me, Pauline. I know you're trying to help, but I won't use the crown as a method of keeping our citizens quiet."

My sister's fists curled at her sides for half a second before she relaxed them. "Right. Never again. Sorry, Jewel."

Her friend bounced back, more self-assured than before. "I knew you were kidding, don't worry about it. So, this fisherman. He's coming after us now, right?'

I adjusted my tail, shifting uncomfortably at her spot-on prediction. "How did you know?"

"Your face when you swam past us. It looked like he was chasing you and you were terrified he might hook you right in the—"

"It's not like that!" I claimed in Randy's defense. "He's trying to find me so he can get to the witch that took Sebastian."

"Hm. Still devoted even after he finds out you're half fish. Maybe I should dump my fin-man and find myself a human, after all."

We laughed, letting the sound ease the tension from the water around us. "Somehow, I think you'd be a bit much for a human male to handle," Pauline teased. "Glad to see you're still feisty as ever, Jewel."

"That I am! And since I'm back on royalty's good side, I hate to be *that* mermaid, but we're headed south. Shouldn't we turn around?"

I shook my head. "Atargatis is south of the Keys."

"Well, duh! I swam here alone, remember? Obviously I know how to get back. Shouldn't we swing up to the ice and pick up your sister?"

"You said Angelique is in Finfolkaheem," Pauline protested. "That's all the way up by Scotland."

"That's a pretty big detour," I agreed.

"Right, but I don't know if that sea witch is still hanging out in our kingdom or not. I was gone before she was."

"Well, she certainly wasn't in Atargatis last night. She was in our apartment."

"She could've gone back to wait for you. We've got a better chance at winning this if Angelique is with us."

"Say she *is* there and has claimed the throne for herself. Our citizens could be suffering under her as we speak. We should check on their well-being first."

"Look, I didn't want to be blunt about it but here goes: You can't defeat her, Fawna. Not by yourself. You saw what kind of magic she's capable of on land, just imagine what a force she is in the water, in her element."

"Fawna is the best sorceress among us," Pauline interjected. "If anyone stands a shot against this new threat, it's her."

"But your mother made sure Fawna's powers never grew, didn't she? None of us were allowed to practice magic, even if it was our gift."

As much as it turned my stomach to admit it, Jewel was right. When I was just a merling, I showed a knack for magic, but Mother was quick to put out that spark. Any mermaid known to practice magic, the queen herself being the exception, was punished severely. No threat to the crown would be tolerated, not even from her own daughter.

"I just... I feel guilty abandoning them. They could need our help."

"If you're so intent on checking on them, maybe Pauline and I should head up to get your sister while you—"

"No," I cut her off. "I told you what that wretched thing said. I've entered the water in search of Sebastian, which means she's after Pauline now. I'll be damned if my sister is leaving my side."

Pauline swam to me, wrapping her arms around my torso and squeezing tight. "It's going to be all right, Fawna. We'll find him."

"Yes," I said with finality. "We will find him. Together."

Jewel caught a strand of her blue hair, tucking it back into place. "Well, I've said my piece, but of course it's your call. Which direction, Your Majesty?"

I thought on it for a moment, considering our options. As strong and fast as we were, the three of us could easily make it to Atargatis by nightfall, but then what? Jewel made some sense; it would do our fellow clan members no good if we charged in, unprepared and lacking skill and strength.

Finfolkaheem, on the other hand, was much too

far away to swim there. It would take us a week at best to cross the ocean. By the time we arrived, Angelique no doubt would have received word by other means of Atargatis's destruction, and we'd miss each other when she rushed home.

We'd need a faster way to get there.

"Well?" Pauline asked. "What should we do, Fawna?"

I pointed a finger toward the surface. "We go up. Randy's boat must be nearby. We haven't gone far. If we flag him, we can hitch a ride."

My sister's eyes went wide. "Maybe you can, but I can't! My necklace is gone, remember?"

"You're going to ride in the bait tank."

"What?" Jewel and Pauline both screeched in union.

"Listen, I don't see any other way to get there quick enough without killing ourselves. Pauline, you and I are out of shape if you haven't noticed. We've barely made it offshore and we're panting already."

"But in the bait tank?" Jewel shuddered. "Might as well ask her to jump on a hook while you're at it."

"Don't be so dramatic. It'll be just like having her own private piece of the ocean to herself. Besides, I happen to know he refilled the tank this morning. With squid. Lots and lots of squid."

Pauline licked her lips, rubbing her stomach at the thought. "I could go for some squid."

"I thought you might." I laughed. "You've never turned it down yet."

Jewel scrunched up her face. "You don't think you'll get claustrophobic shoved inside a little fish tank?"

"Mother used to trap me inside clams as punishment," Pauline reminded her. "I think I can handle it."

"Good," I said with a nod and began to ascend. "It's decided then. Let's hope we haven't missed him."

We broke through the surface, the jostle of the waves knocking us around. The sea was still unsettled. Usually, our tails were strong enough to keep us steady against the churn of the current. I couldn't blame the ocean, knowing how she felt about my abandoning her terrain. To add insult to injury, blood now poured into her, saturating her waters just to the south. It was up to us to stop the hemorrhaging.

Tuning in, I removed the sounds of the water from my line of focus, trying to pinpoint a motor. When ships would sink during Mother's rule, we employed this technique to search out the screams of the survivors. To extract one particular noise from the chaos around us was no easy feat, but with practice and time, it became second nature.

In the distance, and coming closer, the grinding of a tired inboard motor careened toward us at reckless speed. Through the spray of the white caps, I barely caught a glimpse of the approaching vessel in time to point it out and yell for the other two mermaids to get out of the way. Thrusting my tail as hard as I could, I leaped out of the water like a great white targeting its prey, my arms spread wide and waving for attention.

Randy's eyes found me, and he jerked the steering wheel to the right, narrowly avoiding impact as my body fell back into the water.

"For crying out loud," he hollered over the motor. "Fawna, I could've run you over!"

I flashed him my most charming smile. "I knew you'd get it under control. Come closer, I'm getting in."

He brought the boat over and cut the engine before lowering the ladder, holding out his hand for me to take. "I didn't think I'd ever find you out here."

"You wouldn't have if I didn't want you to. Do you have my necklace still?"

"Of course." Randy dug into the pocket of his shorts, pulling out my medallion to dangle it in front of me. I took it from him, then draped it around my neck as I used his grip to hoist myself out of the water.

Before our eyes, my shimmering silver tail melted away. Starting at my knees, milky white skin tore through the scales, the mutation spreading quick until I could stretch and wiggle my human toes. I examined them, pleased at their familiarity, though noting the nail polish I had so carefully painted on just a few nights ago was long gone.

I shook out the pins and needles before climbing to my feet and crossing the boat to lift up one of the seats, revealing a storage compartment. Thank goodness I kept a few spare sundresses in case we made dock somewhere to eat or explore and I needed dry clothing. I rummaged through the assortment, choosing a strapless blue cover up for me and a bright yellow, floor-length piece for Jewel, who

43

still swam somewhere beneath us. Pauline wouldn't need one, I realized as I searched for another garment, since her tail wasn't going anywhere.

"You going to fill me in?" Randy asked once I was clothed.

"We need you to take us somewhere. How much gas do we have?"

"The tank is full, plus I have a couple spare containers tucked under the center console. I'll take you wherever you need if it means getting Sebastian back, but who is *we*?"

"I'm sure you've probably guessed Pauline is a mermaid, too."

"Obviously."

"So she's coming, along with a friend of ours. Jewel."

"Another mermaid."

"Right. Oh! The sea witch that's responsible for this mess destroyed Pauline's amulet. She can't change back into a human."

"Oh man." Randy's grey eyes fogged over, emotion boiling in them. He brought his sunglasses down to cover them, the muscles in his neck pulsating. I slid my arm around his shoulders to bring him close for just a moment. This was a lot to ask anyone to take in at once, and I couldn't have asked him to be more incredible than he was. My heart fluttered as he hugged me tight against him, leaning into my comfort.

"We can't just leave her here," he protested, bending back just enough to observe my face.

"Pauline? Of course not. She's going to hitch a

ride, too. Just... in your bait tank, if that's all right."

Shaking his head, he pinched the bridge of his nose and chuckled. "Mermaids in my bait tank. Man, if you'd have told me when I woke up this morning this was how my day was going to end up, I'd have called you slap-shot crazy."

CHAPTER 6

"You doing okay back there, Pauline?" Randy turned away from the helm to steal a look at my sister, whose white knuckles curled at the edges of the live well, grabbing on for dear life.

The bow of the boat slammed down on the rushing white caps, a salty spray splashing over the sides, all but flooding the deck. A violent rush of wind hurdled toward us, spinning the entire vessel as if we were caught in a whirlpool.

My sister squealed a sound something between terror and pure adrenaline-induced excitement. Jewel stooped down, stuffing her head between her knees. Her blue hair crusted around her face, little bits of vomit sticking to the strands. She dry-heaved one more time, her pitiful eyes begging me for some relief.

"I don't remember seeing anything on radar about a tropical system out here." Randy's eyes darted across the sky, fear sparking afresh with every new lightning strike. "This is like a full-blown hurricane."

Stinging rain collided with the tender skin around my eyes. I ducked for cover, seeking shelter behind the plexiglass windshield. "I don't think this is a natural force at work here. It's too sudden, too strong. Something tells me there's a supernatural influence on the water."

"You're right. This is just like when I snagged that mermaid, only ten times worse."

"She's trying to stop us from reaching Angelique."

"Let her try. We'll fight the weather the whole way if we have to."

"Even as powerful as this creature is, there must be limits to her reach. I'd wager we'll reach calmer waters if we keep heading north."

At the revelation, Randy gave the motor all the power he could, thrusting the throttle forward and into high gear. We sped ahead, crashing through the waves instead of climbing over them. Jewel concealed her face in her forearm, hiding from the breakneck speed as best she could. I crouched down, crawling across the deck. The rough carpet bit into my shins, burning and scraping, but I ignored the pain.

Once Jewel was within reach, I brought her to me. She shifted, eagerly burying her face into the crook of my neck. I rested my chin on the top her head, humming the way I used to soothe Sebastian. We rocked back and forth with the boat, using the rhythm instead of fighting against it. Slowly, her breathing returned to normal, the panicked sobs subsiding.

Poor Randy stood valiantly at the wheel, refusing to give way to the fear I was certain must be beating in his heart. As I coddled a homesick mermaid adapting to being outside her element, he fought the fury of the entire sea without so much as flinching.

I only had a moment to admire his bravery before the sky turned a shade of ominous green. A twisted bolt of lightning spidered across the horizon, and the jarring clap of thunder that followed rumbled in my chest. In an instant, my body lurched forward, suddenly airborne.

Jewel screamed as gravity stole her from my embrace. She reached for me, but the same force tumbled her across the boat's deck, the opposite direction. Flying through the air, streaks of white and blue flew by, my stomach churning as I flipped head over feet. I listened for some sign that Pauline or Randy survived whatever struck our boat, but my efforts were met with an unnerving silence.

My jumbled mind just barely registered the sight of the water funnel plucking our vessel from the ocean just as easily as one might pick a flower from the earth. Now, eerie creaks and cracks popped in my ears as the hull caved to the wind pressure. I hurtled onward, flying about the boat like a ragdoll, shifting direction as the unnatural vortex jostled us about. Just as I thought I might collide with the starboard wall, the boat flipped sideways, dumping us into the angry waters below.

Bitter cold stabbed at my skin like millions of knives. I gasped at the sting, my still very human lungs filling with freezing ice water. Pain nipped at my chest and the salt burned my eyes. On instinct, I coughed out, sucking in another round of destructive liquid.

I swiped at the water and kicked my legs, trying to find the surface again to take in a life-saving breath. My obscured mind couldn't reconcile what was happening; I'm a mermaid, I thought. The acting Queen of Atargatis. Yet the water assaulted me with a furious vengeance, seeming intent on taking my life. Why couldn't I *breathe*?

A heavy darkness pulled on my consciousness, dragging me under. Through the fog, the shadow of Pauline coming closer brought me some comfort. If I was to die, at least I would do so with my sister nearby.

She reached forward, fumbling with something in front of me. When she jerked down, something pinched the back of my neck. The small pain was enough to distract me, enough to regain some clarity. Pauline held up the amulet she had just removed from my neck. In my panic, I forgot the magical necklace still rested on my person, keeping me from changing.

Now, as the slits formed along the sides of my neck and my knees fused together, oxygen pumped through my veins. The saltwater absorbed into my body as the human breathing apparatuses dissolved within my chest cavity, no longer needed. As much as I wanted to take a moment to calm the rush of adrenaline still coursing through every cell in my body, a horrible truth sent me swimming in circles.

Randy couldn't just take off a necklace and breathe.

"Wait a minute!" I froze in place, taking my sister by the shoulders and holding her out to search for damage. The witch was after her now that I'd set out on this fool's errand. Pauline was my first priority. "Are you all right?"

"I'm fine," she answered with a nod. "Jewel is, too. Her medallion was off before she even hit the water. I've never seen a mermaid so happy to be in the ocean."

"Thank Poseidon."

"Where are we? It's so cold and dark here. This place is nothing like Atargatis."

"We must be close to the islands. I'm sure Randy will have a better idea about our location, but we have to find him first. Stay close, okay? It's murky and tinted; I can't see as well as I'd like."

I took off toward the sea floor, certain his human legs couldn't fight against the current any better than mine could. Maybe a little better, I realized. He was born with the things, after all, and a fisherman by trade. Still, he would be no match for these treacherous conditions.

As I asked, Pauline followed, close on my tail. "Jewel is already looking for him," she explained. "If she finds him, she'll bring him top side. We should check there first."

We could swim the entire ocean and cross each other a hundred times this way, I realized. Stopping mid-swish, I stilled. For the first time in ages, I channeled my telepathy, calling out for Jewel.

Over here, I heard in a faint voice to my right. *And I've got him.*

"This way," I called over my shoulder.

Even in the ocean's turbulent blue, Jewel's stunning hair shown like a lantern, guiding me toward the man who risked everything to help me. To help my family. The sight of his limp body in her arms stunned my heart, stopping its beat long enough to ache before kicking on again with a thunderous roar.

I boomed the fork of my tail, one flick pitching me ahead enough to grab a fistful of his shirt and swim upward with all my might.

"Stop!" Jewel shouted. "There's not enough time, Fawna. He's taken in too much water. The only way to save him is to..."

"Don't say it," I warned with a threatening glare. "I'm not going to condemn him—"

"To what, life? Because if you don't, you're condemning him to death."

Pauline gave my elbow a gentle tug. "She's right. You have to change him or he's going to die."

A lump formed in my throat, choking me. Everything was happening so fast; seconds whizzed by me, taking the people I loved with them. First Gene, then Sebastian, and now... As much I hated to admit it, they were right. If I didn't kiss Randy, change him from a human to... something between what he was and a merman, I'd lose him forever.

"With Aunt Myrtle gone the change will be permanent," I argued with myself aloud.

Pauline was the first to counter. "We'll figure it out, Fawna. Aunt Myrtle wasn't the only sea witch in the ocean. If we can't find a way to return him ourselves, we'll search out someone who can. At least he'll be *alive*."

"Oh, for the love of Poseidon." Jewel huffed, pushing my sister away from me. "I'm not going to just swim here and watch him die. You kiss him, or I will."

"Don't touch him," I hissed through my teeth. If any other mermaid changed him, he'd be bound to them forever. A natural, primitive reaction the mind has when one has saved your life, often dramatized as magical. I didn't care for any mermaid, myself included, to hold that kind of power over Randy.

I let out a line of bubbles through my pursed lips and nodded, silently praying Randy wouldn't resent me half as much as I resented myself for having to do this. Closing my eyes to hide from the deed, I pressed my lips against his. And destabilizing dizziness swirled in my mind, winding and snaking around my steadiness until I saw stars. White hot heat combusted where our skin touched, a sensation not altogether different from when I brought Gene down to Atargatis. It was unique, though, and much more pleasant this time around. I knew Randy; I loved him, and my body knew it and reacted accordingly.

This familiarity made the transition much less draining as a piece of my life source transferred over to him. Our beings didn't fight one another for the upper hand. Instead, his energy invited mine in. Magic seeped between us, leaving behind a buzzing residue as I pulled away.

He should've fainted then, if he weren't already unconscious. This was the part where shock took over, sending the human's body into a scramble as it tried to adjust to the sudden changes. The blue would withdraw from his cheeks as the gills traced their way into place. His body would seize up for a few minutes, confused by the sudden rush of water when he took his first breath of sea. I couldn't watch it, any of it.

I opened my mouth, prepared to ask Jewel to bring him to the safety of the sea floor until he woke, but I felt him stir just then. I shot the other mermaids a questioning glance, wondering what in the ocean was happening. When Gene turned, he slept an entire night before he came to. As far as I knew, that was the ordinary aftermath of such a traumatic experience. But, I was the elder here. They shrugged their shoulders, just as clueless as me.

His glassy eyes opened wide, darting around to take in his whereabouts. Once he realized he was underwater, he expelled all the liquid from his mouth and pinched his nose shut. Kicking his legs, he locked eyes on me and pointed toward the surface, silently begging me to bring him up. I shook my head. It killed me to do it, but I urged him to breathe.

"It's okay," I told him. "Don't hold your breath or you'll pass out again."

Randy cocked his head at me, not catching my meaning.

"Look." I took his hand away from his nose, moving it to feel just under his own jawline. "See? You have gills."

His mouth fell open as he ran his fingers along the newly opened seam. My gaze fell to my tail as I prepared for the onslaught of accusations. Gene called me all sorts of names when I turned him; a witch, a mutant, a kidnapper. In Gene's eyes, I could see all of those things in myself. I couldn't stomach seeing that reflection again in Randy's.

Jewel and Pauline drifted away, allotting us space I wanted no part of. The farther they drifted away, the more I fidgeted, anxious and terrified. "I'm sorry, Randy," I offered just above a whisper.

"You're sorry," he echoed, swallowing hard. "What... what happened, Fawna?"

"The boat turned over in the storm. You almost drowned. I swear, Randy, I never would've done it if there was any other way to save your life." My voice cracked, and shimmering tears pooled in my eyes, blinding me. Mermaid tears seemed so unnatural to me now; I had almost forgotten the way they glittered the color of aquamarine.

He took a breath, wobbling in place as he adjusted to the weight of the water around him. I let him go as he asked, "What exactly did you do to me?"

"This is why I couldn't kiss you goodbye on the shore. When a mermaid kisses a human, he's bound to the sea forever. Those gills on your neck, they're permanent. I'm afraid you can't go home."

"What about the necklace you wear all the time?"

I shook my head. "That only works on mermaids. You're not a merman, you're a human under a spell."

"Spells can be broken, right?"

"The only creature in the entire ocean, as far as I know, who knew how to create the antidote was my Aunt Myrtle. She helped Eddie get home after Pauline changed him."

"You said your aunt was dead."

"She is. I'm so sorry, Randy. It was selfish, I know,

but, I couldn't lose you, too."

"Don't apologize, I—"

"I swear to you, I'm going to do everything I can to find a way to send you back."

"I believe you."

I sucked in a rush of air through my flapping gills. "You do?"

"Of course." He smiled, then brushed a strand of silver hair floating in front of my face. "You saved my life, after all. I trust you."

Searching his face, I found no hint of bitterness or insincerity. Instead, complete and utter devotion shined bright in his eyes. "I can't believe you don't hate me."

"Hate you? I could never hate you! Remember, before you tried to take off on me, I told you I wanted to see your world."

"And now you're stuck in it," I reminded him.

"At least I'm with you. I don't care if we're on land or under the ocean; heck, we could be stranded on the moon for all I care. All that matters is I'm with you, Fawna."

The magic in his words sent a shiver chasing up my spine. I buried my face in his chest, grateful for his understanding, though still filled to the brim with angst. It could be the hold I had on him now that made him so deliriously infatuated, but none of the other humans my clan turned accepted their pull so soon. With Gene, he had been submerged for weeks before he came out of his shell. Maybe, just maybe, Randy meant what he said.

I peered up at him, hesitant to accept such hope.

"We should continue toward Finfolkaheem. Angelique has made many friends across the ocean, I'm told. Perhaps she knows someone who can help us."

"I'm not going anywhere until I know Sebastian is safe."

"No, Randy. This isn't your fight."

"The hell it isn't. I love that little guy like he was my own son. What kind of man would I be if I took off and left him in the hands of the monster that took him?"

"Exactly that — a *man*. You don't belong down here. The plan was you would deliver us to the drop off point and leave."

"Plans change, my sweet. This one took a hard left the second you turned me into whatever I am now."

"Stop being so stubborn. You have no idea what you're getting yourself involved in. My mother was as fierce as sea witches come. I've witnessed first-hand how brutal dark magic can be."

"Great. So you'll be a fantastic tour guide."

"Randy!"

Jewel popped up between us just as I raised a hand to shove him away. "Sorry to interrupt your little lover's quarrel, but it's getting dark out and my tail is freezing. Can we just get to Angelique and figure this out later?"

"That sounds like a great idea," Randy agreed with a grin.

I huffed, scowling at the obstinate two-legged interloper. "Fine," I seethed through gritted teeth. "How far are we from the islands?"

"About a hundred miles or so. If we just keep heading northeast we should hit them fairly quick."

"Good." I raised the fork of my tail. "Grab hold."

Randy's brows shot to the top of his head. "You want me to hitch a ride on your tail? No way."

"Boy this sounds familiar," Pauline said with a giggle. "Eddie and I had this same debate when we were looking for Aunt Myrtle."

Unlike Pauline, I would give no leeway on the matter. My son's life and the welfare of my entire kingdom were at stake. "Do you want in on this mission or not? Because I'll leave you here and come back potion in hand once I've found a way to make it. There's no way you can keep up with us, I don't care how great of a swimmer you are. You'll slow us down."

This time, it was Randy clenching his jaw and wearing a glare that could spear a lobster. "Fine."

CHAPTER 7

"This is your kingdom?" Pauline marveled at the magnificent crystal fortress.

She hovered to look out the window, mesmerized by the glowing coral and plant life in the garden below. Despite the colors around us, everything in Finfolkaheem carried the distinct appearance of freezing death. Tiny ice crystals formed on the palace, lingering to remind us just how vulnerable everything this far north was to the elements — and yet, there was a beauty in it all.

This place resembled Angelique's detached elegance, fitting her perfectly. I could think of no kingdom better suited to her rule.

Above us, a thick glacier disguised the finfolk's home, making it all but invisible to the humans who fished from the surface. An ingenious use of nature. If one didn't know what they were looking for, they'd never have a clue that an entire civilization lived just under their vessels.

"Yes," Angelique responded, pride blooming in her cheeks. "Lennox was elected by the citizens to serve as king. He accepted, only on the condition that I could rule by his side as an equal. A female equal to a male, quite the far-fetched notion in these waters, but I haven't met much opposition."

"Sure beats the heck out of the palace in Atargatis," Jewel said, admiring the structure.

"There's nothing wrong with our palace," I scolded. "Or anything else about our kingdom."

"I didn't mean anything by it, just that this palace is huge. Our whole kingdom could fit in here!"

"It's a beautiful place to call home," I told Angelique, who sat perched on her throne with the most regal posture I'd ever seen her wear.

The new queen observed us carefully, her welcome anything but warm. Perhaps the cold water of the north chilled her heart, or maybe she knew our presence here brought only bad news. Either way, I clasped my hands in front of myself, mirroring her business-only demeanor. This wasn't quite shaping out to be the warm reunion I had been hoping for.

"Thank you." Her words were clipped and suspicious. When her gaze flicked to Randy, I understood the reason for her apprehension. Angelique was never very fond of humans. "You all traveled a long way to find me. And you brought a human, no less."

"How could you tell him apart from the fin-men walking around?" Pauline wondered.

"Like the fish and seaweed in my kingdom, the fin-men glow. Didn't you notice when you passed them by?"

A soft blush painted our younger sister's cheeks. "Oh, yeah. Everything around here seems illuminated. I guess I just thought it had to do with the environment."

"You're not far off. It's the residuals of King

Odom's magic. I imagine it'll be a few hundred years before it wears off entirely."

Randy shifted in place before taking a timid step forward. "I know you."

Her chocolate brown eyes roamed his person from top to bottom, and a sudden flash of recognition made the muscles in her face pull tight. She recoiled, blanching as if he had thrown a bucket of chum in her royal face.

"You!" Angelique pointed an accusing finger in Randy's direction. The crown set atop of her head trembled as her face turned a deep shade of raging red. "You're the human who pulled me up in a net."

"What?" Pauline shouted. "You hooked my sister?"

Jewel flew forward, placing herself mere inches from Randy, ready to take him down in an instant. He held out his hands, palms to the sky, and she turned her anger to me. "I thought you said we could trust him?"

"We can," I insisted.

"I knew this was a bad idea. We should've made this trip on our own; we didn't need his help."

"Listen," Randy started, "It was a long time ago, and it was a mistake."

Angelique waved her tail out in front of herself. "I don't care if it was a mistake. Look what he did to my tail!"

I examined the fork of her fin, my stomach clenching when I saw the faint white outline of a scar running up the center of it. At some point, and apparently by Randy's doing, the edge of her tail was split down the middle. Just imagining how painful it must've been to swim with such an injury made me shudder.

Even Randy winced. "Ouch. How did that happen? It was just a net, I never hooked you."

"Oh, I don't know. Thin skin tends to tear pretty easy when you plunge twenty feet from the air and smack a crazy pissed-off ocean at full speed."

"Oh man. I'm really sorry, I never meant—"

"And did you or did you not threaten to put me on display?" Angelique demanded. "Use your unevolved species' mythology behind my people to make yourself a quick buck? Because the money you make off the thousands of pounds of fish you steal from the sea isn't enough. You're lucky my Lennox is away on a hunt or he'd strike you down where you stand."

Randy waved his hands out in front of him, warding off her attack. "Whoa, whoa. You're right, okay? It was a terrible thing for me to do. But, in my defense, it was Reggie's idea. My captain at the time. He was the one who wanted to—"

"But you were going to go along with it."

"I was considering it," he admitted. "I'm sorry. There's no excuse. If it helps, I've felt guilty about it every day since. It was a bad judgement call on my part. Now that I know what I do, about you and the other mermaids, I'd never even think about treating you in such a despicable way. You're not a fish, I get that."

Angelique narrowed her eyes on him, weighing his explanation and apology. "Damn right I'm not a fish. Either way, human, I'm not sorry to see you stuck down here. In fact, I'm rather enjoying seeing you as far outside your element as you were witness to me outside of mine. If you're lucky, I won't instruct my men to trap you in a net the way you and your captain did to me."

A small smirk lifted on the edge of Randy's lips. "I won't be much help to your cause if I'm tied up."

My sister leaned forward, her chin pointed and stern. "I don't take help from humans. Jewel is right; they should've left you behind. Whatever my sisters and friend have come to discuss with me does not concern you. Now, will someone please tell me why you brought this stinking creature into my kingdom?"

"Randy is my... um," I stumbled, unsure what to call him.

"Your human?" Angelique asked, raising a sharp, manicured brow. "Don't tell me you've resorted to Mother's old tricks. Scavenging ship wrecks to get your power trips? I suppose next you'll drag him up to the surface to watch him air out."

Randy paled, pulling at the collar on his soaked t-shirt. "Jesus, that's down right evil!"

"Yes," she snapped. "It is evil. And though I consider the practice outdated and archaic, I may be willing to make an exception to my distaste for it if the victim is you."

"He's not my victim, Angelique." I pressed my backside into Randy's chest, finding his hand with my own and intertwining our fingers. "He's my boyfriend."

"Ugh. You too, Fawna? I thought for sure you'd get sick of being around them so often, but here you go attaching yourself to one."

"What's wrong with choosing a human mate?" Pauline challenged. "It's worked out well for me."

"That's right... Eddie," Angelique sneered.

"What's your problem, Angelique? You and Jewel both chose fin-men, didn't you? Of all mermaids, the two of you should be able to look past such little differences."

Angelique threw her head back, cackling at Pauline's sudden burst of bravery. "It's not the human part I take issue with, dear. She's choosing a fisherman. His profession makes him an enemy to the entire ocean."

"Hey," Randy protested. "I'm no one's enemy. I don't fish like Reggie did. Now that I'm the captain, we only take enough to maintain a living. I'm not trying to get rich taking your food."

I squeezed his hand, and Pauline added, "See? He's good. Just like Eddie."

"Speaking of Eddie," Angelique said with a sigh, "where is the headstrong little human?"

My sister crossed her arms in front of her chest, suddenly looking guilty and withdrawn. "He's at home."

"Didn't care to join you on your trek across the ocean this time?"

"He... doesn't know I came. Eddie would want to come if I told him, and I didn't want to put him in danger again."

"Because of what's happened in Atargatis."

I cocked my head at her, surprised. "You know?"

"Of course I know. Jewel's boyfriend, Ainsley,

went to see her. When he returned, he told me it looked as if a bomb was set off in the center of the city."

"Oh Poseidon, no." I rubbed at my chest, willing the ache to dissipate. The thought of my kingdom in such disarray tore me to shreds. "Did he speak of survivors?"

"He brought a few back with him."

"May I speak with them?"

Angelique shook her head, her face hard as stone. "I've tried. They're shell-shocked. Whatever trauma they endured was enough to silence them entirely. They won't speak a word; not about Atargatis or anything else."

"The poor mermaids." Pauline gasped, covering her mouth with the palm of her hand. "They must've seen something horrific."

"So it seems. Jewel, Ainsley has been in mourning since he came home. When he couldn't find you..."

"He thought I was among the lost." Jewel's body stiffened. "Angelique, may I excuse myself to find him? I have to let him know I'm all right."

For the first time since our arrival, my sister's expression softened. Swimming up from her throne and in our direction, she waved her hand toward the exit, shooing the blue-haired mermaid to it. "We'll catch you up on what is decided here. I can only imagine he'll be all too pleased to see you're alive and well. Go to him."

"Thank you."

"But take the stinking human with you."

"Randy stays with me," I argued, but Angelique

warned me with a single look. One very reminiscent of our mother. I had to remember, this was her kingdom. As long as we swam in these waters, Angelique was our queen.

I bowed my head in apology, observing her status with as much respect as I could muster for the mermaid who, once upon a time, was but second in line for the throne — behind me.

"You may be willing to risk our secrets for this... human, but he has yet to prove himself to me. I won't discuss this any further in his presence."

Randy rested a hand on the small of my back. "It's okay, Fawna. I understand she doesn't trust me yet. I could use some rest anyway. It's been quite an eventful couple of days."

"Good. Jewel, you'll find Ainsley in his quarters. Tell him I require his assistance in settling Randy into his own room, then the two of you may have the day to yourselves."

Jewel didn't waste a second before she snatched Randy's wrist and dashed out. With them gone, I turned back to the queen of Finfolkaheem. As much as I resented her treatment of Randy, I couldn't exactly blame her. If he had caught me in a net and threatened to cash me in, our relationship would probably have gone in a very different direction.

"Have you any idea who would want to attack Atargatis?"

"Just about every clan in the ocean, I suspect. The brutality behind Mother's reign did not simply disappear because she no longer wore a crown."

"What about capability," Pauline questioned.

"There can't be many who possess the kind of magic we saw in the apartment."

Angelique threw a questioning glance between Pauline and me. "An apartment is like a grotto, only on land," I explained. "It's where we lived."

"Right. I think you've mentioned something about it before when I brought Sebastian to you. Where is my nephew, by the way?"

"She took him," I answered, blinking back the tears that threatened at the mention of his name. "Whatever this... creature is took my son."

My sister's nostrils flared. There was no need to say it, she blamed me for this. I shriveled under her condemning stare, suddenly realizing how much I shared that opinion. "You should've left him with me."

Without a defense, I merely nodded. Guards swarmed the halls of Finfolkaheem. To reach Sebastian, that witch would've had to cut through them all. If nothing else, it would've slowed her down; tired her out enough for us to find her. Because of my selfish maternal need, I brought him to a world without magic, a world where I couldn't protect him no matter how much I wanted to.

"It wouldn't have mattered where he was," Pauline contended. "Blaming Fawna isn't going to do anything but make the situation worse. She feels bad enough as it is."

"The first and only merman in our family is gone, kidnapped at the hand of a mad witch who will do Poseidon knows what to him. Make no mistake, sister, she should feel badly."

"Our sister is right," I acknowledged. "The blame is mine and mine alone. I accept that. My son is gone because of my poor decision to bring him into a world where he didn't belong. Considering how special he is, I should've predicted someone would come after him. Now, Queen Angelique, what do you propose we do about it?"

"Before we can decide how to proceed we must find out who is behind this mess in the first place. You called the kidnapper a she. What makes you think it's a female?"

I lifted my shoulders. "Maybe it's just because I'm still not accustomed to considering males among our kind. After all, as long as I lived in Atargatis there weren't any mermen at all. But, this witch possessed Jewel, and there was something very feminine in her energy."

"Possession? That is a unique skillset."

"Not only that," Pauline added, "she sucked the magic out of my medallion."

Angelique opened her mouth, stunned for a moment. "You're saying she broke through Myrtle's magic?"

Our youngest sister nodded fast and sharp. "That's right. I would've died if it wasn't for Jewel and Fawna rushing me to the ocean."

"Neither of us has any knowledge of the clans outside of Atargatis," I explained. "You're the only one who has a rapport with outside species."

She clucked her tongue, and I could almost see the smart retort fighting to escape her lips. No one could blame her for reminding us that this particular predicament was our own doing; that if we had stayed in the ocean after Mother's fall and acted as Ambassadors of our kingdom, maybe we'd know more about the dangers of the underwater world.

"There's only one sorceress in all the oceans who I'm aware of having such advanced magical abilities, but I don't care to speculate."

Pauline snorted. "There's not much else we can do at this point, is there?"

"There may be. We have a fin-man here, we call him Gilcrest. He possesses his own ability similar to what our clan called precognition, only much more versatile. More than simply see the future, he can see almost anything."

"So, he's a psychic." Pauline bobbed up and down, her black hair bouncing behind her.

I held up a hand, cutting off her excitement. "You said almost anything. What are his limitations?"

"The sea uses him as something of a conduit. Gilcrest can only see what the ocean wants him to."

"Well, then let's hope she's on our side in this battle."

CHAPTER
8

Gilcrest was strange looking, even for a fin-man. His ears pointed to the sky, oversized and not at all fitting to his tiny head. He looked... alien almost, with a slight yellow tint to his skin that shimmered with the passing current. The sleeves of his seaweed green robe covered his hands, which he clasped in front of himself as he bowed to my sister.

"Thank you for agreeing to meet with us, Gilcrest. I know you prefer your solitude."

"I prefer silence," he corrected, glancing up before sweeping his gaze across Pauline and me. "Solitude is just one way to ensure I go undisturbed."

"At any rate, we appreciate you making time for us."

"If you require my assistance, then you might ask your guests to stop gawking. It's rude."

Pauline's eyes darted to the floor, and I pressed my palms against my cheeks to cool the heat stinging them. "Forgive us," I pleaded, "this is the first time we've been to an underwater kingdom outside of Atargatis. We're not accustomed to seeing creatures that look... well, there's no polite way to say it, is there? Like you."

Chuckling, Gilcrest's stomach created a wave

of its own as it jiggled. "You could search the whole ocean and never come across another creature like me."

"I beg your pardon?"

"I'm something of a hybrid, a cross between the merrows and finfolk. A collection of genetic material collided not so beautifully to make this."

Angelique huffed and rolled her eyes, making a show of her annoyance. "I've heard the pity story before, Gilcrest. The ocean punished you by making you hideous, then made up for it by granting you this marvelous gift."

The psychic's face twisted, his jaw clenching tight. "It's an enthralling tale of the ocean's justice. What a pity you've denied them of it. I tell it much better, I promise you."

Pauline giggled, the magical sound lightening the air in an instant. "I'm certain you do. I'd love to hear it from start to finish when we're not in such a hurry."

Gilcrest stepped toward her, brushing her pale face with the backside of his knuckles. "Such innocence. Such beauty. Quite the contrast to the cold company so often found in this part of the ocean. You, I prefer to your sister."

I pressed my lips together, biting back a smirk. He wasn't the only one to prefer Pauline to Angelique. As I anticipated, Angelique screeched out her disapproval in one ear-splitting squeal. As agitating as the sound had always been to me, I couldn't help but let myself feel glad that this chilly environment hadn't managed to cool her red hot temper. She was still Princess Angelique under that fancy new title.

"How dare you?" she shouted, swiping her tail against the ground in a furious fit. "I brought you here to use your gift, not to ogle my land-loving sister."

"Jealousy is the root of that nasty disposition of yours, Queen Angelique."

"Don't be stupid. I'm not envious of her or anyone else. I'm impatient. We're in the middle of a crisis, Gilcrest, and we need your help."

The arrogant, smug look in his eye faded, as if he realized as well as I did how hard it was for Angelique to admit to anyone that she needed help. "All right, Your Majesty. I'll do what I can."

"That's all I'm asking."

"You need to know who has assaulted your people." It was a statement, not a question. It caught me off guard. He truly was gifted to see so much already.

"Do you know who it was?" I blurted out. "Can you see the sea witch or find a motive?"

He squinted, pressing his fingertips into his temple to massage tiny circles into the side of his cranium. "Not clearly, no. The sea, she wants to show me, but there's something blocking the vision."

"She's created interference," Angelique said with certainty. "Whoever it is knew we would turn to Gilcrest's gifts."

"Can you see anything?" Pauline urged. "Maybe a symbol in the static or anything at all that could give us a clue."

Keeping his eyes closed, he shook his head. "Something... something keeps undulating by. A snake, I think."

Angelique sucked in a sharp breath and reached to me for stability. I allowed her to rest her weight against me, holding up both our weights with my fanning tail. "That's significant in some way," I prodded.

"It means my fear is realized." Angelique shivered, then wrapped her arms around her torso. "We're not dealing with an ordinary sea witch. This is Mami Watta, keeper of the damned souls lost at sea."

Pauline whimpered, inching closer to us. "She sounds terrifying."

"How in the name of Poseidon do you know a mermaid who watches over the dead?" I wondered, trying to talk over the goose pimples popping up along my arms. "What kind of people have you been making friends with while we've been gone?"

She pulled away from me, squaring her shoulders and preparing to defend herself. "She's not what I would call a *friend*. I met her on my first voyage to Finfolkaheem. Stumbled into her, really. Mami claimed to be a healer, a protector of the ocean."

At that notion, Gilcrest laughed again, shaking his head at the absurdity of it. "The only thing that witch cares to protect are her silver and her snakes. To the ocean's depths with anything else."

"You know her, too?" Angelique asked, genuinely curious.

"Not in person, no. She's been the subject of many of my less savory visions. One could say I know her through divine introduction."

"But you haven't actually seen her in this vision,"

I pointed out.

"No, however I do lean toward Queen Angelique's interpretation. As I mentioned, there's the bit about the snakes, but whatever field she's using to block my full view of these events bears her energy signature."

"I'm right," Angelique maintained. "I know Mami Watta's magic well, and this whole thing reeks of her dirty work."

Pauline rested a concerned hand on Angelique's shoulder. "Did she hurt you?"

"No, no," Angelique assured her. "But, she did tell me she was in league with Mother just before she had her merman-killing spree. They had a falling out."

"A bad falling out," I guessed.

"Brutal. Apparently, Mother sentenced her to babysit the dead for eternity. She can never die or, as far as I was told, leave her little corner of the ocean."

"Well, it seems she's found a way around her imprisonment."

"It certainly looks that way."

Pauline was the one to ask the question the rest of us were too frightened to voice aloud. "So, how can we stop her?"

Three pairs of eyes landed on the seer, expecting. If I were in his shoes, the weight of the pressure would've hunched my shoulders, but his experience allowed him to wear it well. Bringing his hands back in front of him, he breathed in deep through his nose, then out slowly through his mouth.

"I make no promises," he warned, and the lot

of us nodded our understanding. "This will require great concentration to break through her barrier. I require complete silence."

We gave it to him. Each of us tightened our mouths until our lips turned white, watching him as he closed his eyes to block out the world and its distractions. The water around him vibrated. The ground quaked just beneath his feet, the crystal floor cracking at the tips of his toes. He let out a grunt, then barreled over, clutching his stomach.

I moved my fingers toward him, seeking to soothe his obvious discomfort, but Pauline swatted my hand away. She whipped her head from side to side, mouthing no. Against my maternal instincts, I pulled my arm back. When he heaved himself upright again, we jumped back, startled by his abrupt movements.

Gilcrest's eyes snapped open, and he narrowed his line of vision on me. "This is your battle to fight."

My breath hitched in my throat. "Wh... what?"

"Your sisters are all but useless here. Their gifts cannot begin to rival Mami Watta. Only you have that power."

"You're mistaken. You saw wrong, you must have. I don't have any power at all."

"My dear, I saw your lineage. You're the first born of the fearsome Queen Calypso. Of all her children, you have inherited that gift of sorcery by right."

"You call it a gift while my mother claimed it a curse! Whatever powers I inherited from my mother I don't know how to use. How could I be any match for a sea witch who has practiced for centuries?"

He stared blankly at me, telling me all I needed to know. Even he, the great seer of the seas, didn't have all the answers.

My fingers and tail tingled as blood rushed to my extremities. Every cell in my body came alive, the instinct to swim away almost undeniable. I couldn't face this sea witch, not on my own. I was nothing more than a dethroned princess whose magical abilities had been deliberately stunted since birth, and yet the fate of all the oceans depended on me winning a battle I didn't want to be in.

How could I just swim away?

Gilcrest cleared his throat, pulling me from my indecision. "You want to know about your son. His part in all this."

A single tear broke through my barrier, lifting into the waters as a shimmering speck. I wasn't sure I was brave enough to endure his answer, but before I could stop myself I was down on bended tail, pleading.

"Yes. Please, tell me anything. I need to know my son is still with us."

The hybrid patted the top of my head, pity etched in the deep lines around his yellow-tinted face. "Sebastian lives. Mami Watta intends to use the magic inside his tiny beating heart to break the seal of her own fate. Only through his blood can she destroy the curse that binds her here. Once she is free, Mami Watta can use her ability to shapeshift and spread her evil like a plague among the land and sea alike."

"She already has the ability to travel between land and sea," I argued. "Mami snatched him from his cradle. She came to our home on land."

"All is not what it seems, young princess. You cannot always trust what you think you see."

"I was there! She possessed Jewel then nearly killed my sister."

"What you met of the great sorceress was nothing more than a projection of herself. She stretched her spirit while her body stayed behind. In such a state, her powers would be severely stunted."

The color drained from Pauline's cheeks and she said, "If she's capable of such magic while her abilities are limited, just imagine how strong she must be in person!"

The look of pure terror crossing my little sister's face fed into my fury. This witch and her treachery were responsible for Pauline's fear. Half of my family was missing, while the other half cowered together. It was unacceptable, and I wouldn't stand for it.

My lips trembled and my hands drew into fists. "I'll kill her. Whatever it takes, I must strike her down before any harm comes to my baby. She won't take his life, I won't let her!"

"Time is running out. She will perform the ceremony at the next full moon, on the shores of Morocco. You have two weeks, young mermaid, not a night longer."

"Tell me what I need to do."

"The only way to succeed is if you're willing to delve deep into a world you've been taught to fear. Magic must become an extension of you, a burden you take on willingly and without complaint. To reject it is to fail."

"I would gladly do as you suggest if it meant saving Sebastian, Gilcrest, but I have no way to learn the art of sorcery. My aunt has perished, and my mother is missing."

"Your mother isn't missing, she's a prisoner, and you must fight for her, too. Mami will not kill her; even she fears the pure evil that pollutes Calypso's blood, but the fallen queen will be left to rot in the world between the living and the dead if she goes without rescue. As far as Mami Watta is concerned, the only threat to her plot is your mother. That's why she took her. To prevent her interference."

"I know who can help you," Angelique interjected. "I've made a friend nearby, a merrow named Margaret."

"Ah ha!" Gilcrest lifted a sure finger toward the sky, as if the idea were the most brilliant he'd ever heard. "A merrow is exactly what we need. The miracle-makers of the sea, they are. And I'm not just saying that because I'm half one myself."

I licked my lips, tasting the salty brine of the ocean around me. Before today, I had never heard of a merrow, but if she could help save us from falling at the mercy of this wretched sea witch, this Margaret would be the most valuable ally in the sea.

Suddenly, the entire palace wobbled, and a familiar dark energy descended in the kingdom. Pauline held out both her hands, grabbing for Angelique and myself.

"She's here." Gilcrest's voice shook, and my stomach turned at the spark of complete terror on his face. If this seemingly unshakeable hybrid was afraid of her, I should be terrified.

"You must go," Angelique ordered. "Gilcrest, open a portal."

"A what?" I looked between them, confused.

Gilcrest shook back his sleeves, waving his hands in front of himself to form a large circle. The water followed his movements, whirling in on itself until a contained vortex formed.

"Go through," Gilcrest told me, but I still waited for Angelique to go forward first.

"This will open directly into the kingdom of the merrows." Angelique pushed on my shoulders, edging me toward the rift. "My place is here in Finfolkaheem. I can't rule from afar, not while Lennox is away."

"I can't just leave you!"

"She'll leave once she senses you're gone, I'm sure of it. Mami will come searching for you, sister. Be sure you're ready to receive her."

"But, Randy! I can't abandon him, either."

"Your human is safer with me. At the moment, I'm the one with the guards. I'll see he's looked after well."

"Hurry," Gilcrest urged. "I can't keep it open much longer!"

My tail twitched, I was ready to swim between worlds when Pauline caught my eye. Remembering the sea witch's threat, I yelled one last desperate plea before proceeding. "Don't let Pauline out of your sight. The witch has her net set on Pauline as well."

"We'll be fine. Go!"

CHAPTER
9

As soon I swam through the gateway drawn by Gilcrest, my tail flipped over my head. My body careened forward, caught in the clutches of an unnatural, swift current. The thrust shoved me along as though I weighed little more than a minnow, and I flopped around as ungracefully as a catfish on the deck of Randy's fishing boat.

I opened my mouth to scream, but the deafening sound of rushing water whisked the noise of my own voice away. When Angelique urged me through the portal, I assumed I'd swim right into the kingdom of the merrows, not find myself swirling around the ocean along an underwater thrill ride.

The sudden acceleration threw bile into my throat. Green at the gills and ready to vomit all over this Poseidon-awful creation of the fin-men, I forced myself to arch my back and tighten my core to stop my disorganized flight pattern. I ran my arms in long circles as I tipped upright again, wobbling in place until I regained my balance.

Once I was sure I wouldn't fall forward again, I took a moment to figure out what kind of contraption that trickster half-breed sent me into. A tunnel, I realized. A tunnel that acted like a roaring river, cutting through the ocean's depths. It carried me to my destination at such incredible speed, I almost couldn't see the bright and colorful coral and marine life that sped by outside of the underwater highway.

My stomach contracted again as the motion around me sent my head spinning. I pressed the heels of my hands against my eyes, rubbing until the sensation passed. Just as I brought my arms down again, my nausea found itself replaced with a sweeping sheet of dread. The end of the tunnel was in sight, but this portal showed no signs of slowing down.

I whipped myself around, swimming as hard as I could against the current until every muscle in my body burned. It was no use; even the strength of a mermaid's fin was no match for this vortex. Craning my neck, I could only watch as I punched tail-first through the other end, soaring into calmer waters like a bullet. A vibrating boom exploded all around me, my ears aching from the sound.

Nimble hands took hold of my arms, and the joints in my shoulders popped as I came to a sudden stop.

"Catch your breath," a female's voice cooed at me.

The image of her in front of me swayed and tripled. I closed my eyes tight and shook my head, trying to will away the dizziness. A strange figure crossed itself a few times, multiplying and merging again until finally just one creature remained. She resembled Gilcrest, I realized, though not quite as hideous. *A merrow.*

While she didn't glow yellow, her scaled green skin took me aback. The pigment matched a strand of detached seaweed that had been beaten and smudged by the elements. Her enlarged pointed ears overshadowed her stringy unkempt hair. Black beady eyes watched me, wide with concern, and I decided I wouldn't allow her unpleasant appearance to make me falter the way Gilcrest's had.

Swooping myself upright, I faced her with a warm smile. "I'm all right. Thank you for watching over me while I recovered."

The woman giggled, covering her mouth as her amusement escaped. "That was quite the landing."

"I'm afraid I entered that transport tunnel in a hurry. I didn't have time to ask the hybrid who made it how to navigate it properly."

"And I'm sad to say I must rush you along again. We must hide you before anyone else notices you've arrived."

"We?" I asked, pulling away as the merrow grabbed at my hand. "Why should I hide myself? I'm searching for a merrow named——"

"Margaret. That would be me. Angelique told me to meet you out here. Bad timing as I was in the middle of a council gathering, but she said it was urgent so I excused myself."

"I'm sorry, I'm a little confused. How could Angelique have alerted you to my arrival so quickly? I only just left Finfolkaheem."

Margaret pointed to her temple, tapping it with her wart-ridden finger. "Merrows are telepaths, too, though I've never met a mermaid who could extend her reach as far as Angelique. When she wants your attention, she makes sure she gets it no matter where in the ocean you are."

"She was always very gifted in that regard. Telepathy was her power. The gift of song belonged to our youngest sister, Pauline."

"I've heard. Nabbed a human on her first hunt. I'd say how unfortunate, but it seems to have worked out well for her."

A gentle smile lifted my lips, and I inched closer to the merrow. "You seem to know a great deal about my family."

"Angelique and I have become good friends. Which is why I agreed to help you hone your talent, Fawna."

"I'm not sure I would call it a talent."

"The ocean has told Gilcrest it is, so it is. You just need an introduction. I'm sure you'll catch on in a flash. But first, we really must conceal your arrival. The less witnesses we have, the better."

Margaret swam forward, waving me along. I followed, quickening the strokes of my tail to match her pace. "You speak as though my being here is trespassing. Am I not welcome? I can leave if my presence causes you any distress."

"Don't be silly," she insisted. "I'd never turn away Angelique's sister. It's just... I don't exactly have permission to harbor you. The merrows have something of a peace treaty with Mami Watta."

"I can't imagine what cost such a bargain would come at! From everything I know of her, Mami is a wretched, vile cast-off of the sea."

"Oh, that she is and more. But, she gave us an offer we couldn't refuse. See, she wanted to alter the dead she looks over, give them the ability to venture on land to sell goods every full moon. We have a spell book in our keep, one that contained such forbidden magic. She attacked us repeatedly to get at it, sending troops of the undead to our door to do her bidding. You can't kill a ghost with just anything, and the poisons required are costly."

"I could only imagine the ingredients such a potion would require."

"Finally we had to make a choice: give her the one page she wanted or chance her killing every one of us and getting her hands on the whole book."

"That couldn't have been an easy call to make."

"I thank Poseidon every day I wasn't yet alive to be the one to make it. I'm the High Priestess, after all. It would've been my call, just as bringing you into our kingdom for asylum is now."

"The High Priestess," I repeated, the term foreign to me. "Does that mean you're in charge of your clan? Like a queen."

"Nothing quite so dominating. I oversee the magical happenings among my kind. It's my duty to keep the ancient spell books safe, and that responsibility comes with a bit of authority."

I bit my lip, tossing around Margaret's earlier comment about hiding me. Guilt nagged at me, and I realized even without knowing the whole story, this ally of my sister was risking her good stature by taking me in. "Your clan wouldn't approve of my arrival. That's why we're sneaking around the ocean."

"Not because they don't want to help you," she rushed to reply. "It's only because of fear. They wouldn't want to provoke Mami Watta."

My blood went cold, and I stopped swimming in an instant. Somehow through the excitement of my arrival and meeting this new friend, I hadn't even considered what danger my presence could bring upon them.

"They would be right to want to keep away from this conflict. Mami Watta will follow me here."

Margaret turned around, realizing only once I spoke that I no longer swam beside her. "She wouldn't think to search here for you. No offense, but until recently we weren't exactly keen on the mermaids that came from Atargatis. Your mother spilled a lot of blood, and the pollution of her sins spread even this far. We felt her evil every day when she ruled."

"She'll sniff me out." I dragged my fingers through my hair, pulling at the white strands as if the slight sting would bring me comfort. "Mami Watta found me in Finfolkaheem."

"Right, because she knew you'd swim straight to your sister. Everyone knows she rules beside Lennox now. Our relationship isn't common knowledge, and we prefer it that way. The best ally is a secret one."

I glanced over my shoulder, back in the direction of the magical tunnel and murmured, "I hope they're all right."

"Angelique told me Mami disappeared almost as soon as you did, like she knew you left. She's probably searching the ocean for you as we speak, so again, we need to get you hidden."

Shaking my head, I backed away as Margaret

swam toward me. "I can't put the merrows in danger. No one else should suffer so I can hide like a hermit."

"Look," Margaret swatted her tail, "as admirable as I find your self-sacrificing nature, this isn't just about your clan. The sooner Mami Watta is gone, the better the whole ocean will be for it. The sea has chosen you to defeat her, and to do that we need to work together. Please, for the good of everyone, let me help you."

I crossed my arms loosely in front of my torso and drew in a ragged breath. She was right, I knew as much, but it just didn't feel right putting an entire kingdom of innocents in jeopardy. The only way this would work is if my lessons were carried out in absolute secrecy.

"Who else knows I'm here?" I asked, flicking my gaze around.

"Not a soul. I figured the fewer merrows that knew, the less mouths that could reveal your whereabouts."

"Good thinking."

"I'm not exactly new to this whole secret mission thing, Fawna. There's a reason your sister trusts me."

"I don't doubt your skill or loyalty for a minute, High Priestess."

"Good. Let's get moving then, shall we?"

We swam in silence, hugging the barren seafloor until the waters warmed just enough to chase away the remaining chill from Finfolkaheem. How Angelique managed to survive in such frigid temperatures was beyond me. Our bodies were built for the warm, lush waters of the tropics, not a freezing world beneath a huge iceberg.

Night was closing in fast, swallowing up the few rays of sunlight that remained, yet in the distance hundreds of glowing orbs caught my attention. I slanted my head at them, mesmerized by the brilliance. Nothing in Atargatis illuminated so bright, not even Mother's concoctions inside her cauldron.

"That's it," Margaret beamed. "The Kingdom of the Merrows."

"Stunning. I can't believe you found a way to bring electricity all the way down here."

The merrow scrunched up her nose and shook her head. "I don't know what electricity is. Some human thing I'm sure. They have the strangest names, I swear. Those are orbs of concentrated magic. Makes life a lot cozier down here when you can see a couple inches in front of your nose."

"I imagine that's so. It's quite the ingenious use of your powers. The Finfolk would certainly benefit from its use. Their kingdom was dreadfully dark and depressing, at least compared to what I've grown accustomed to."

"Angelique and I have discussed the possibility of trading. Poseidon knows we could use some additional protection around here, and fin-men are the ocean's most adept warriors. But, we feared the arrangement might bring attention to our newfound allegiance, and we didn't think it worth the risk."

"Even with your so-called peace treaty your clan seems to live in great fear."

Margaret nudged my shoulder with hers, giving me a playful shove. "You're going to fix that for everyone. I can feel it."

I forced a fake smile. Though I was grateful for her vote of confidence, the road ahead would not be an easy one. Two weeks. I had two weeks to bring down the ocean's most powerful sea witch and bring peace to every child of the sea. This feat, I realized, would not come without significant struggle. The thought alone made my shoulders sag with exhaustion, and I covered my mouth to yawn.

"You're tired," Margaret observed aloud.

I stretched my neck back, banishing the ache that set itself into my bones. "I haven't slept in a couple days. I'll be fine. We should start my lessons right away."

"You won't be much use to the cause if you're too tired to control your reflexes. Once we get to my grotto we'll turn in for the night. We can start preparing first thing in the morning."

A protest formed on my tongue, but I swallowed it down. The merrow was right. She knew far better than I how much energy would be required in the next couple of days. I needed to set my pride aside and heed her advice.

As we entered the kingdom, I was surprised to find their walls were nothing more than a chiseled out cavern. As the scattered orbs flickered, haunting shadows danced along the rock walls, giving life to the sharp edges and archaic foundation. Such a magically-advanced species could no doubt construct structures far more elaborate than these, but the design itself made sense. Without the light created by their magic, this kingdom would appear to be nothing more than an underwater cave. Uninteresting to any would-be trespassers.

The only way in was through a singular wide mouth, guarded by a thick iron gate. The slats dug deep into the sand, preventing any intruders from simply digging their way in. Fearing the sound would alert others to our arrival if we opened it, we shimmied our slender bodies through a pair of wide slats and continued down a narrow entryway, which opened wide in the center.

A lone table sat in the center, long enough to seat several dozen merrows. Countless tunnels and corridors, also clearly merrow-made, ran deeper into the cave system. One wrong turn in this room alone could render one completely lost if they didn't have the layout memorized. I opened my mouth to ask where the others in her clan were, but Margaret pressed a green finger to her lips.

I nodded and kept close, following the merrow down one of the tunnels on the north side. A dozen doorways lined the hall, each covered with plain wooden doors. From inside one of the rooms, a female giggled and the doorknob jiggled as someone swung the door open. My breath hitched in my throat, and Margaret snatched my hand and launched us both forward until we came to the last doorway.

She shoved me in, closing the door behind us and waving a hand over the frame. Something clicked, the sound reminiscent of a deadbolt securing in place. Margaret pressed her back to the door, as if her body provided an additional barrier between me and her clan. "That was close," she said, releasing a hard breath.

"I'm surprised you don't have your own quarters given your status."

"We used to separate the classes. The servants lived in and maintained the lower quarters, commoners in the middle. Only royals were housed on the top floors. Much like King Odom's set up when he ruled Finfolkaheem, the higher the level, the higher you were on the clan's hierarchy."

The Fin-folk employing servants I could see; by first impression, they appeared intoxicated by power. But the Merrows seemed far too advanced for such backward social practices. Margaret must've read my shock, because she was quick to add, "We don't use servants anymore."

"That's good to hear," I admitted. "I'm ashamed to say the humans even beat Atargatis to the revelation of the barbarity of slavery."

"I insisted on the change as soon as I returned from King Odom's captivity."

My jaw unhinged, falling open. "You, the High Priestess of the Merrows, were captured by King Odom?"

"It's true. That's how I met your sister. He was unaware of my title, but I served under him for quite a while. Sometimes I think it was a blessing in disguise. The experience taught me a strong lesson in humility. That's why I moved my quarters down here."

"I'm sure that was a tremendous adjustment for all of you."

"Well worth the effort. We're all much happier as

a whole."

Her positive outlook on her own personal tragedy struck me as admirable, and I found myself smiling at her. "I'm glad to have met you, Margaret. You're a wonderful friend of the sea."

"Likewise, Queen Fawna. It is queen now, isn't it?"

I bit my lip, still unsure of the title. "I suppose it is. Although, I'm afraid I'm just as clueless about ruling a kingdom as I am about how to wield magic."

"Well, I can't help you on the queen front, but I can help with the magic bit. *After* a good night's sleep."

CHAPTER 10

I woke up alone in Margaret's quarters, curled up on jutted bedrock. The morning brought more brightness; the natural rays mingled with the artificial light of the scattered orbs, providing a clearer view of the merrows' grotto. Stretching my tail, I propped myself up on my elbows to scan the room.

The similarity between Margaret's room and my mother's old hidden chamber of magic was remarkable. Antique books lined the walls in disorganized heaps. Artifacts and magical charms scattered the room, and in the center, a bubbling cauldron stinking of sorcery. The only thing missing were the maps marked with red X's to pinpoint the enemy's whereabouts.

Swimming over to the black pot, I examined the heated liquid it held with a shudder. I didn't know what kind of potion brewed inside it, only that I wanted no part of it. Mother's concoctions always brought about suffering, and my only experience with this kind of magic brought back a sickening feeling of guilt and shame. I played a hand in her treachery, willingly or not, and this place reminded me of that more than I cared to allow.

"Oh good. You're awake." Margaret called from the doorway.

I startled, wondering how she managed to sneak up on me. This was no time to let my guard down, and I made a mental note to focus on every single sound I heard going forward. Every whoosh of water, every creak in the walls, I had to be aware of it all. The enemy would not sneak up on me. There was far too much at stake to be so foolish.

"Good morning, Margaret," I said, clearing my throat.

"I hope you slept well."

Nodding, I responded, "Very well, thank you. If you'll permit it, I'm ready to begin my lessons. Where do we start?"

"Someone's eager." Margaret laughed softly, shaking her head. "It's still so early! All right, lesson one: breakfast."

At the mention of food, my stomach released a hideous gurgle so loud I was sure every merrow in the kingdom heard it. Somehow, through all the excitement, not only had I forgotten about sleep until it was called to my attention, but sustenance as well.

"I guess breakfast does sound good," I admitted with a sheepish grin.

"Thought it might." Margaret removed a satchel I hadn't noticed she was carrying from her shoulder and pulled out a handful of uncooked squid tentacles.

Saliva pooled under my tongue, and the bitter taste of bile rose in the back of my throat. Raw squid. I hadn't eaten raw squid since I moved my life landside, or raw anything for that matter. Pauline savored the tradition, ordering up a heap of uncooked sea-critter every time she had sushi, but I'd long since decided I preferred it battered and fried.

Not wanting to seem ungrateful, I swallowed down the excess liquid building in my mouth and held out my hand to take her offering. Margaret threw her head back and cackled. "Your face just turned a few shades of green. You could almost pass for a Merrow."

Whatever green-hue she referred to must've disappeared in that moment, replaced with the burning red embarrassment now scalding my cheeks. "I guess I managed to get hooked on human food in the time I spent on land."

"I prefer seafood cooked, myself. Especially squid. The tentacles are hard to get down either way, but it's a little easier when they aren't so... chewy."

"You've had cooked squid?" I perked a brow at her, curious about how she could've had the opportunity.

"Sure." Margaret kept her collection of raw cephalopod to herself, taking it over to the cauldron. "I have no idea how the humans cook it, but maybe this will help." She dropped the handful of flesh into the simmering potion, stepping back as it sizzled. "This won't take but a minute."

She fetched a long spoon from a nearby table, then dipped it in to stir her concoction before hoisting our breakfast back out. Crispy golden strings made my mouth water, this time without the acidic taste of disgust. The smell of delicious deep-fried goodness wafted over to me, making the rumbling in my stomach go haywire.

"That's amazing," I announced. "It looks just like calamari."

"Cala what?"

"It's fried squid. The way the humans cook it. That looks delicious."

"Oh. Glad I could get it so close."

"You cooked that with magic?"

"Well yeah. Magic doesn't have to be all doom and gloom. Just like the orbs that give us light, we enjoy using our powers to make life more enjoyable in general. Food is a big part of that, at least for me."

"Margaret, you're my kind of merrow."

She snickered, then held out her hand. "Down here, though, they get soggy in a heartbeat. The magical barrier can only stay in place so long. Eat up before the water breaks through the crunchy shell."

She didn't have to tell me twice. As fast as she could plop a handful in my palms, I transferred the bits to my mouth. Recognition and satisfaction settled in my stomach. The flavor and spices were absolute perfection, almost an exact recreation of the calamari Randy and I enjoyed at our favorite restaurant.

I stopped mid-chew at the thought, the taste sending a wave of nostalgia through me. The same ocean-side diner we said our first hello and almost last goodbye, and we ordered calamari every single time we went there. For me, it was the perfect balance between my home on land and my home in the sea. The combination reminded me of myself, a good mix of both worlds yet still a part of each.

Randy never understood why I enjoyed it so much, but he indulged me none the less. Now that he knew who I was and where I came from, I was sure he would connect it the next time we got the chance to eat there. If only he were here to enjoy it with me now. A sweeping sadness buried itself beneath my skin, clinging to my insides and coating them with a regret so penetrating I wasn't sure I could ever shake it.

I left him. Almost as soon as I dragged him into this world without his consent, I abandoned him in a kingdom strange even to me. This time I didn't even take the time to bid him farewell. And now here I swam, enjoying one of our favorite meals like this was a vacation while he no doubt struggled to understand my sudden disappearance.

Good Poseidon, I prayed Angelique would be kind to him. She wasn't exactly team human, and the last thing Randy needed right now was someone treating him like a trespasser of the ocean.

In silence, I finished the remainder of my breakfast without the same pleasure I started it with. Margaret watched me, concern creasing the faint wrinkles between her eyes, seeming to sense my inner turmoil but granting me the kindness of keeping my struggle to myself. This wasn't something she could understand, and I believe she knew as much.

"Now then," she said and waved her hands against the still water to brush away the bits of magical-breading still clinging to her fingertips, "what kind of magic do you know how to do?"

I blinked at her. "None. Mother forbade it. Though, when I was a merling, I did set an entire coral reef on fire while I was having a tantrum."

"Oh, this I have to hear."

"I'm not sure how it happened. One minute I was screaming because my mother's guard wouldn't allow me to explore a shipwreck, the next thing I knew, a big ball of fire exploded from my hand."

"All by itself?" she marveled with a chuckle. "That must've been some surprise."

"I remember thinking it was the coolest thing. If I could shoot a fireball under water, what other tricks could I show my friends in powers class? But, Mother got so angry with me. She told me in no uncertain terms that, princess or not, if I ever used magic again she would exile me."

"And you never tried to use it again?"

"Never on purpose. It slipped out a time or two, usually during sibling squabbles. My sisters swore they would never tell." The side of my lip quirked up just a little at the memory. "They never did, either."

"That doesn't surprise me. I've found Angelique to be very reliable as far as keeping her word."

"I can't argue that. We haven't always seen eye to eye, but she does keep her promises."

"Right. Now, we know you have the fire in you, speaking literally. Let's let it out. That fear Queen Calypso put in you? Let go of it."

Preparing, I stretched my neck from side to side, lifting my hand out in front of me. Margaret squealed and swatted it away. "Don't point it at me!

You could catch me on fire."

"Sorry!" I flinched, then recalled my hand, holding it against my chest.

"It's all right, just aim at the wall."

"What if I strike it? The whole castle could collapse."

"You're in a kingdom full of magical merrows. We teach our young how to handle their magic the same way I'm teaching you, which means our buildings have to be impervious to magical catastrophe, or our particular brand of it, anyway. You won't breach it."

I chewed on my lip, considering her claim before deciding to try again. Again, I lifted my arm, pointing my palm toward an empty wall across the room. My shoulders tensed as I squinted, burning a hole in the foundation with nothing more than my stare. Letting out a disappointed groan, I turned back to Margaret.

"Nothing's happening."

"You're still afraid of it. Your subconscious isn't letting your power come through. Let the wall down, and the magic will flow naturally. Now, try again."

Unconvinced, I did as she asked. Thrusting both my hands forward this time, I held my breath and pushed with all my mind's strength until I went cross-eyed. Nothing more than bubbles formed from the disturbed water dancing around my exasperatingly normal fingers.

"Come on, Fawna," Margaret urged. "Find the wall around your magic and tear it down."

In a fit of frustration, I threw my hands in the air and shouted, "How can I break through a barrier I can't even see?"

"Of course you can't see it! You have to feel for it."

"I don't feel anything." My confidence dwindled, leaving an ache in my chest as it waned. For the first time since hearing my fate, I wondered if I could actually pull this off. "Margaret," my voice came out pitiful and strained, "what if I can't figure this out?"

She shrugged, not seeming to care one way or the other. "Then people suffer and die, just as they do every single day. Look, if you can't do it, you can't do it. Don't waste your time fishing for the impossible."

"What?" My jaw dropped. "You can't be suggesting I throw in the anchor already. We've only just started, and I thought you said you would help me!"

"You're repressing your own ability, Fawna. I can't help you break through that voice in your head."

"Well... we can't just give up, Margaret! Lives are depending on me figuring this out."

"The success of this little adventure depends on you violating your precious mother's rules. I don't know if you have it in you."

"Are you kidding me?"

"She's still got you wrapped around her tailfin. There's no way you're strong enough to face Mami Watta when you can't even conjure up a simple spell because Mommy said it was against the rules."

Whipping my head from side to side, I argued, "Margaret, you're wrong."

"Did you or did you not murder your one true mate because Queen Calypso ordered it?"

"What?" I swam back as my face went numb. The

reminder pummeled into my gut, leaving me breath-less. "What's that got to do with—"

"And now you've brought another human down to his death. Say you do rescue her, Fawna. By some miracle, imagine you manage to swim in and save your mother's life. What do you think she will do to your latest human boyfriend when she meets him? Something tells me she's not exactly going to wel-come him into the clan with open arms."

"What my mother thinks about my relationship with Randy is irrelevant."

"Is it? See, this is how I see it going down: Mom-my dearest meets the sailor and just the sight of him will send her into a feeding frenzy. She'll want his blood, out of reflex if nothing more."

"Stop it."

"And you, Princess, won't so much as speak up as she drags him to his death, too."

I gasped, stunned at her audacity. "That's a lie! I would never, ever let anything happen to Randy."

"Forgive my skepticism, Fawna, given your track record."

My track record? I planted my fists on my hips, just above the rim of my tail. Who did she think she was? My sisters and I faced our mother head on. We removed her from the throne, then I went to live among the all-forbidden human race.

My cheeks scorched at her condescension. This merrow couldn't even begin to imagine the things I'd done or the hardships I faced because of who my mother was. My track record spoke for itself. Just as I opened my mouth to tell her so, a small, arrogant smile pulled up on Margaret's lips and she turned toward the door.

"Hey," I yelled, my chest alive with fire. "Turn your tail back around and face me. We're not done here!"

With the command, I threw my fist forward, hurling a grenade of magic in her direction. She jumped back as the fiery orb sliced through the water and jetted past her ear, barely missing her as it collided with the wall.

In slow motion, the supposedly reinforced cave wall cracked, buckling under the power suddenly impacting it. A perfect sphere in the spot where my assault landed slipped out of the wall, the edges so clean it was as if it was cut with a laser. Margaret's eyes widened, but before she could say a word a male's voice boomed in the hall.

"What in Poseidon's name was that?"

CHAPTER 11

In the gaping hole now marring the wall between Margaret's grotto and the outside hallway, a pair of beady eyes set on a peeling green face darted around. The male merrow's gaze froze on my frame, and I shrank back as Margaret sailed in front of me. Her small body barely covered mine, even with her arms outstretched wide.

"Is that a—"

"It's nothing!" Margaret was quick to interrupt him.

The door to her quarters flew open, a burst of bubbles flooding the room. Margaret pressed her back against me, trying to shield me as long as possible. Even when the suspicious male tried to swim above her to get a view from overhead, she swatted him away. His shadow loomed over her, the darkness swallowing me up.

Compared to Margaret, this beast was a hideous sight. Boils covered his skin, and his pointed ears were so massive they made Margaret's look petite. A ragged piece of cloth draped over his shoulders, floating behind him as it caught in the subtle currents in the water. He inched closer, breathing in my scent through his bulbous nostrils. His face scrunched up, as if I was the one who was offensive to the senses. An involuntary shudder came over me before I remembered myself and straightened my spine. He wouldn't intimidate me, not after the incredible magic I somehow managed to let loose.

"This is my grotto," Margaret protested. "I didn't invite you in, Regis. You can't just barge in—"

"After an explosion like that I think I'm entitled." The intruder flicked his fin, sliding past her until he got a good look at me. "What are you thinking bringing a mermaid in here?"

"That's none of your business."

"I think that chunk of rock that came flying out at me makes it my business."

Margaret snorted. "You're always such a drama-fish. That projectile didn't come anywhere near you."

"Answer the question." He pointed a grotesque finger at me. "What's it doing here?"

"It?" I challenged, but Margaret raised a hand to silence me.

"She is my friend."

"Has your choice in allies become so poor, Margaret? I smell Calypso's blood in her veins. Clearly, your time in captivity has left your judgement more than just a little impaired. Why else would a merrow consort with the spawn of that sea-demon?"

"There's nothing wrong with my judgement! You know of the uprising in Atargatis; the entire ocean has heard of it. It's unfair of you to judge Fawna for the deeds of her mother. Besides, she needs our protection."

"She just blasted a hole in the wall! A wall specifically designed to withstand magical assault. Her power sliced through with expert precision as if the wall was made of nothing more than sand! That alone seems to suggest that it is us that requires protection from her."

"It was an accident," I interjected on my own behalf. "I've never used my powers before. Margaret was teaching me, and I sort of... lost control."

"What kind of sea-witch loses control of her own magic?"

"I'm not a sea-witch. My mother was, but I've been forbidden to exercise my abilities."

A slight smirk threatened on the edge of Regis's peeling lips. "Probably because they were afraid you were going to blow up the whole kingdom."

"Very funny." Margaret huffed. "Were there others in the hallway? The less people that know about her the better."

"The clan is out on a hunt. A few of us stayed behind to keep guard. As far as I know, I'm the only one who noticed the damage. At least thus far."

"Thank Poseidon." Margaret breathed out a sigh, her shoulders sinking down in relief. "Fawna, this is Regis. He's one of our clan's most gifted scouts, my brother, and, at least as I know him to be, a trusted friend."

Regis groaned at the not so subtle hint. She was asking him for his alliance, insinuating she expected his silence on my presence. Suggesting that if he was the friend she claimed him to be, he would comply.

"You're a spy?" I inquired. "What is it you investigate, exactly?"

He crossed his arms in front of his chest, leaning back to size me up. "I sniff out the weaknesses of our enemies so that, if need be, we're ready to defend ourselves in the most effective fashion. I inspect anything and everything that might pose a danger to my clan. And right now, Princess, you're my number one target."

"Your suspicions are unnecessary. I mean no harm to any of you."

"We'll see about that."

"You won't say anything, will you, Regis?" Margaret implored him to abide.

Regis eyed me again, this time with his head tilted in curiosity. "That depends. What sort of creature can send the daughter of the ocean's most fearsome mermaid swimming for her life?"

I swallowed hard, almost afraid to say the name aloud. As if the mere mention would manifest her into being. "An enemy we both share. Mami Watta."

He squinted his eyes, seeming confused. "Your mother should be more than capable of fending off her minions. The required spells aren't complicated, only costly. The merrows won't venture into the sort of dark magic needed to defeat her, but Calypso bathes in it. Surely she could offer you safer refuge than we can."

"It's not her undead slaves that are after me. Mami has taken the duty upon herself to hunt down my family."

"You're mistaken, Princess. Mami Watta is confined to her own kingdom by the same curse that charges her with overseeing the dead."

"I wish that were true. She's already taken my mother from her prison in Atargatis, along with my child from our home on land. I was there when she took my son. I witnessed her presence first hand, and it was no ghostly messenger. A seer I met, Gilcrest, claims it was only a projection of her spirit, but her magic was devastating just the same."

A tense quiet filled the room as Margaret and Regis stared at one another, their faces paling to a lighter shade of green. I fidgeted with a scale on my tail, waiting awkwardly for the moment to pass and someone to react. This should be no surprise to Margaret; I told her upon my arrival I was concerned about Mami finding me in her kingdom.

"Say something," I begged.

"Well," Margaret cleared her throat, "this is new information. Angelique did mention Mami's presence in Finfolkaheem, but I just assumed it was one of her undead acting on her behalf."

Regis scanned the room, as if searching for the elusive sorceress in every corner. He lowered his voice to nearly a whisper, leaned in Margaret's direction and said, "If this is true, and Mami Watta has found a way to break her binding, we cannot harbor the mermaid here. Mami would tear down these walls with a flick of the wrist."

"We're not going to just send her to her death! Fawna doesn't stand a chance against such a villain on her own, at least until she harnesses her abilities."

He turned to me again, changing his approach. Taking my hand in his with a gentle squeeze, his eyes begged me to listen. "Try to understand. It's not that my clan wouldn't want to help you, but we can't risk all our lives to save one."

"I do understand," I responded with complete sincerity. "I know she'll attack your kingdom if she finds out I'm here. And I'm not asking for permanent refuge in your kingdom. Believe me, Regis, I don't plan on spending the rest of my life in hiding. There are other members of my family, humans that I care about too deeply to remain here for very long. She'll go after them if she can't find me, and I won't let that happen."

"Then what are you proposing?"

"I have to learn how to wield my own magic. I have less than two weeks now before she performs a ceremony that will claim the life of my son, all to free herself of her limitations. If she succeeds, the merrows will be in just as much danger as my clan, along with every other creature on the face of the earth. Someone has to stop her, and I'm willing to take on the task but I can't defeat her if I'm powerless."

Regis blinked hard then shook his head, processing my words. "You think you can take a few lessons, swim right up to Mami Watta and win a war of magic against her? Forgive me, but Calypso's daughter or not, you'll lose. She has centuries of practice over you. There's no way you can make up for that kind of experience in two weeks."

"I have to try." My voice cracked, but I swallowed against the strain. Now was not the time to show weakness.

Failure was not an option; not if I wanted my baby safe or my sisters alive. My Mother, well, of course I would do my best to save her, but I could recognize a punishment when I saw one. The sea wanted her to pay for her misdeeds, and perhaps this was her way of setting the ocean's karma right again.

Regis rubbed at the creases of his forehead as he concentrated on the floor, lost in thought. "What type of ceremony is she planning, exactly?"

"Don't be stupid, Regis," Margaret snapped. "How would she know that?"

"Listen, all I'm saying is brute magic won't win this. If we knew what sort of spell she was casting, what it entails exactly, maybe we could figure out a way to sabotage it. If we can keep her focused on repairing some other essential part of the ceremony, it might give us an opportunity to save the kid."

"That plan seems sound," Margaret agreed with a sharp nod.

"The hard part will be getting the information we need."

"You're an espionage expert, are you not?" I challenged. "Tell me what to do and I will follow your guidance without question."

"Infiltration. It's the simplest way. If we can sneak into her lair without being detected, we can have a look around. If we're lucky, she keeps her current spell of choice on display the way King Odom did. A nighttime arrival would be best. Mami Watta doesn't sleep, but at least we'll have the shroud of night covering our bubbles."

An uneasiness settled itself on me at the thought of swimming around an unfamiliar kingdom filled with the undead in the middle of darkness. The set up felt like a scene from one of the horror films Randy watched so often. Why he enjoyed the dreadful feeling of fright so much was beyond me. I hated the way the suspenseful music would bring the hair on my neck to stand or the shrieks and cries of the actors would turn my stomach. Perhaps it was because I heard those screams from the mouths of so many real mermaids in Atargatis. The horror scenes dredged up too many unpleasant memories. To Randy, it was just a movie. But to me, it was a trigger.

At any rate, Regis was right. If I was to remain undetected, an approach at night would offer me the best chance. "Okay. I can do it. Do you have a map to Mami Watta's kingdom?"

"You're not going alone," Margaret nearly shouted. "I'm coming with you! I promised Angelique I would help, and I intend to follow through on my word."

Regis ran his fingers through his short, tangled black hair and laughed. "I should be the one to go. Neither of you has any experience with this sort of thing."

Surprised, both Margaret and I turned to him, mouths agape. "Now you want to aide Calypso's daughter?" I asked.

"A moment ago you didn't even want her here," Margaret pointed out. "You were ready to throw her to the sharks!"

He shrugged, a sheepish grin on his face. "The

princess makes a good point. If we let Mami Watta finish whatever evil she has started, we could all be doomed."

"How selfless of you." Margaret rolled her eyes.

"Whatever your reason is," I placed my hand on his shoulder, pushing back the urge to hug my new ally. "I'm grateful for your help. I can't let you go alone, though. The lives of my son and my mother are at stake."

"Then it's settled," Margaret announced. "We'll all go."

Regis grimaced, clearly displeased to have the company, but said, "Fine. But just remember, scouting is my domain. Margaret, you may be the high-priestess, and Fawna, you may be a princess—"

"Actually, at the moment I'm the acting queen," I instigated with a sly smile.

"Fantastic. Whatever titles the two of you hold are irrelevant. Once we're outside these waters and in enemy territory, I'm in charge."

CHAPTER 12

"What do you think her kingdom will be like?" I wondered aloud with a shudder.

"Full of beings and energies never meant for the ocean," Regis answered with absolute certainty in his tone.

He settled against the wall of the cave we had sought refuge in for the night, its location a mere dash from the entrance into Mami Watta's world. While Margaret remained outside hunting, Regis and I took up shelter. A sack hung around his neck, and he swung it around the front of him as he sat on the seafloor. After rummaging inside it, he pulled out a pair of binoculars similar to the ones found on human ships, only the lenses glowed white.

"What are those?"

Regis pressed them against his eyes and peered through them in the direction of the cave's mouth. "For seeing long distances. I want to be prepared for whatever we're up against in the morning."

"No, I mean, why are they glowing? I've seen binoculars before, but those are... different."

"Different is a good thing when you're talking about human contraptions. They build their things to suit them on land, and most of their tools are useless down here." He held them up, pointing to a nearly invisible dome covering the lenses. "We try to find ways to modify what dribbles down here from their world. I'm not sure how they work exactly, I'm a spy not a scientist, but somehow they absorb light during the day to provide a clearer view of things at night when we can't light our orbs."

"Why can't you light an orb?"

"We don't want to lead Mami or her minions right to us, do we?"

I blushed, realizing how inexperienced I must sound to his ear. "I suppose we don't."

He snickered. "Mermaids."

"They're solar powered," I mumbled, aware that the terminology would mean little to Regis. The familiarity in it offered some comfort to me, though, as if talking about humans and their things brought me a little closer to home somehow.

"If that's what the humans call it, sure. Margaret told me you spent some time living with them."

"About a year. A little more."

"I've always wondered what it would be like. Walking, I mean. To be able to move around without the weight of the water on your shoulders."

"To be honest, I still prefer swimming," I admitted. "It's... freer. On land, you're stuck to the floor. You can't dash off in an instant, or twirl around. Well, I guess you can spin, but it isn't the same."

"Bet it's lighter, though."

"Sure, but the air doesn't coddle you the way the ocean does. There's an intimacy missing in the atmosphere. Something to be missed. I spent most nights sitting on my back porch watching the waves, longing to dive in them again. It was fun at first to be on land, but there's nothing quite like home."

"Why would you stay for a year if you missed the ocean so much?"

Resting my head back against the rough surface, I drew my tail up and wrapped my arms around the bend of it. "My sister, mostly. She loves it up there and she's so young. I couldn't bear to leave her alone."

"You must love her a great deal."

"I'd do anything to keep her safe."

"I, uhh..." Regis picked up a rock, tossed it between his hands, then dropped it again. "I heard you have a human male you're fond of."

A soft smile formed on my lips, and I nodded. "Randy. He's a big part of why I stayed as well. He only just found out what I am, where I'm from."

"I bet that was a fun revelation. He probably took off, right? Humans are fickle beings. They're so frightened of what they don't understand."

My love-sick grin faltered at the accusation. "No! Not Randy. Actually, he followed me back. When he almost got himself killed, I had no choice but to..."

"You kissed him."

"And now he's part of this whole mess. His life is in danger now too because of me."

Regis chuckled, the light from his binoculars setting his yellow teeth aglow. "I'd say if he jumped into the deepest part of the ocean to follow you, it's safe to blame love for his predicament, not yourself."

"Maybe. Right now I just want to get him home."

"Will you return with him?"

"What?"

"When this is over. If we win. I'm sure after all he's been through he'll want to go home. No one could fault him for that. But, will you go back, too?"

I blinked at the merrow, unsure of what to say. Of course I wanted to be with Randy, and I knew Pauline needed me with her on land but... my kingdom needed me, too. With Angelique in Finfolkaheem and Margaret gone, I was the only royal Atargatis had left that was fit to rule. Mother would never be accepted back on the throne, regardless of any progress she may have made. That wound would never fully heal.

He read into my silence, and offered a silent, understanding nod. "Tough choice. Make yourself happy and let everyone else down, or abandon the love of your life and live in servitude under the ocean's order."

Opening my mouth, I prepared to agree with him when Margaret burst into the cave, leaving a trail of wild bubbles behind. "We have a problem," she announced, far louder than I would've preferred.

As I shushed her, Regis winced, bringing a chewed up, half-dead-looking finger to his lips.

"Sorry," she whispered, almost inaudible this time. "There's been an attack. Finfolkaheem has gone under siege."

Without command, my body jolted upward as I screamed, "What?" The tender exposed flesh on my back scraped against the jagged cave wall, the sting just barely enough to keep me from teetering into hysteria. Distraction was a powerful ally, but the gravity of her words threatened to throw me into a full blown panic.

The image of the two merrows below me came in and out of focus as I forced myself to breathe. My mind scrambled to calm the ferocious beating of my heart. I left them. Pauline, Randy, Jewel... the only reason any of them were in Finfolkaheem in the first place was because they followed me. It was me who led Mami Watta to Angelique's kingdom, and deep down I knew she would return for me.

And I still left them.

Margaret clasped my shoulders in a firm grip and slid me back down until I floated eye-level with her. "Princess, I need you to steady your breathing."

"What... what's happened?" I stammered. "Where are they?"

"I'm not certain of their whereabouts. While I was hunting I tried to connect telepathically with your sister. Angelique requested regular updates on our progress and I planned to fill her in on our current method of approach."

"And?" Alarm strained my voice, and as I started to topple forward, Regis pulled my torso against his to hold me upright. I let him, leaning against his larger frame for support.

"I couldn't reach her."

"Couldn't that simply mean she's sleeping?" Regis countered. "Think of the hour, after all."

"Angelique is a night fish. She sleeps more during the day than any other time."

"It's true," I agreed.

"I kept trying just in case, but eventually I felt

something... some sort of interference before another voice inserted itself onto our wavelength."

"Whose voice?" I insisted.

"I'm sorry, it was no one familiar to me. A female."

"Pauline?"

"I don't think it was your younger sister. This female sounded older, almost depleted. Like the energy it took to contact me was all she had left."

"What did she tell you?"

"Just as I said: there was an attack. Mami Watta sent some sort of mist to the kingdom, instantly putting every fin-man or otherwise in a death-like sleep. That's why I can't communicate with her. Angelique and the others are unreachable."

"I don't understand," Regis said. "If they're all asleep, then who sent you the message?"

"Someone from outside the kingdom, obviously. Maybe someone who witnessed it."

"Oh Zeus!" I shouted, clutching my stomach. "We have to help them."

"We don't even know where to find them," Margaret argued. "For all we know she left them right there in Finfolkaheem to lure you back."

Regis's jaw flexed, a fury rippling off his body that could rival my own. "No, Mami Watta isn't a new fish to combat. Every move is calculated. She knows she has a greater advantage in her own kingdom, where she can fight as more than just an apparition. At the very least, she took all those relevant to Fawna. Her sisters, her human boyfriend."

"She must've taken them back to her kingdom. We need to go. Now." I swam for the cave's opening, but Regis clasped his fingers around my wrist, jerking me back.

"That's the last thing we should do."

"We can't just leave them at her mercy!"

"Think about it, Fawna. You're a smart mermaid. Angelique and her new clan made no move against her. Why would Mami Watta kidnap them?"

"It's a trap," Margaret announced firmly. "She's trying to lure you in."

"It was probably Mami who relayed the message to Margaret in the first place. Otherwise, she'd have no way of knowing when you might return to Finfolkaheem to discover what she'd done."

I shook my head, refusing to admit the logic in their explanation. "No. Margaret, you said the female sounded weak. Right now that sea witch is anything but weak. She's about to gain more power than any creature in the ocean has ever had."

"Fawna." Regis took my shoulders and turned me to face him. "She's a master in the art of deception. Every single detail you could pick apart, she's painted over. I guarantee it."

"What if you're wrong? What if somehow a mermaid or merrow stood against Mami Watta, put her life in danger to get us that message, and now finds her neck in danger? We can't swim away from the possibility, Regis. Too many innocent creatures have already gotten hurt."

"Do you remember what I said before we left?" Regis puffed out his chest, his cheeks turning a darker shade of green. "I'm in charge out here, you agreed to it."

"I respect you and your experience, I do. But... Regis, we're talking about my sisters. That old hag has already taken my son and my mother away from me. There's a very real possibility I may never see either of them again, I understand that as much as I hate it. But, Pauline and Angelique as still within reach. Don't ask me to abandon them."

Regis crossed his arms in front of his chest, raking his gaze along my face with a scrutiny that made my skin tingle. I lifted my chin, a regal defiance shaping my posture until my shoulders spread and my back went rigid. He chuckled, shaking his head.

"Another stubborn queen. Just what the ocean needs."

"I rather think so," Margaret chirped. "Even if you are being a sarcastic ass about it."

"All right, Fawna. We'll go to Mami Watta's kingdom, but we follow the original plan and wait until nightfall. End of discussion."

"It is nightfall, Regis."

"No, it's the middle of the night. We're all exhausted and hungry and nobody can think with a clear head while they're struggling to keep their eyelids open and their stomach quiet. We'll eat, sleep the rest of the night and stay in hiding tomorrow until dusk."

"You want me to wait until—"

"Didn't I say end of discussion already? If you want my help, if you want to survive this to help anyone, then this is how we attack. Got it?"

As much I wanted to continue the debate, I needed his help. Alienating Regis would be a grave mistake. I clamped my mouth shut, swallowing the argument that scorched my throat, and nodded my assent.

"Finally. Now, Margaret, how was the hunt?"

CHAPTER 13

"Holy Poseidon." I peered through Regis's adapted binoculars, blinking hard to make sure I wasn't imagining what I saw. "Are those... ghosts?"

"The souls of the undead," Regis confirmed. "Trapped here to do Mami Watta's bidding."

"I heard the rumors but I thought it nothing more than legend."

Our bellies grazed the ledge of a cliff overlooking a crevice, at the bottom of it was Mami Watta's kingdom. A jutted rock just in front of us provided cover as we scoped out the terrain, paying close attention for obstacles and threats.

Regis pressed a piece of parchment against Margaret's back, making notes with glowing magic-tainted ink. "They're as real as us. Half alive and held prisoner."

"What are they doing down there?" Margaret asked.

I shrugged. "I don't think they're doing anything. Swimming in circles, it looks like."

"Look closer," Regis urged. "Any detail could be significant."

I inched around the boulder and leaned over the

ledge a bit more, trying to get a closer look. Distorted figures, or rather their silhouettes, wandered the kingdom aimlessly. A red and white cloak covered the shoulders of each of the spirits below, but the moonlight cut through their visible flesh, as if they were made of nothing more than mist and shadow. Every one of them wore the same haunted look on their nearly transparent faces as they swam along, glancing down on occasion to scowl at something.

Following their forlorn stares, I found the roads beneath their wispy tails to be in ruin. Fragments of blasted coral littered the ground. Piles of discarded lumber lined the ocean floor, the very presence of the clutter seeming to cause the spirits distress. I zeroed in on a piece of wood, intrigued by burn marks on its surface.

The char-marks branched off in zigs and zags, with spider-like extensions pointing in all directions. The marks resembled a bolt of Florida lightning, beautiful and entrancing, yet deadly and unforgiving. Chaos in its most hypnotizing form.

"It looks like a bomb went off down there," I murmured. "Like all the buildings were set on fire. The... things keep looking at the wreckage."

"Let me see." Margaret swiped the binoculars from my hands and brushed me aside to take advantage of my hidden look-out point. Almost instantly, her mouth turned downward and her green skin paled a shade.

"Margaret," Regis said, "what is it?"

"Those scorch marks... that's the residue dark magic leaves behind. Mami Watta must've destroyed whatever structures once stood there."

I shook my head, flicking my tail to inch back just enough to regain a sense of safety. "That doesn't make sense. Why would Mami destroy her own kingdom?"

"Looks like the ocean's most powerful sea witch had a temper tantrum to me," Regis said.

"That's one hell of a tantrum. She demolished the place!"

I wrapped my arms around my torso to banish a shudder. If she was capable of this kind of destruction when it came to her own kingdom...

"Maybe her minions wouldn't obey," Margaret suggested with a twinge of hope hanging on her words. "That would set her off for sure."

Regis quirked a pointed brow at her. "That's awfully optimistic."

"Hey, dead or not people can only be beaten down so much before they have had enough. The entire ocean knows that Mami Watta's brutality outshines even Queen Calypso's. No offense, Fawna."

"'Have you any idea how much tyrants fear the people they oppress...'" My voice trailed off, and I garnered some curious glances from the merrows around me. "Sorry, it's a quote from one of Pauline's favorite books. In any case, Margaret may be on to something."

The male merrow scrunched up his nose and threw his arms up in exasperation. "How do you figure? All we have to go on is a pile of rubble in the middle of a mad witch's kingdom. That doesn't exactly scream revolution to me."

Margaret shoved the binoculars at him. "Look for yourself, Regis. Their expressions alone tell the story. They're heartbroken, looking at every piece of debris as if their lives went down in flames with their homes! The only thing left standing is that sorry excuse for a castle that Mami tucks herself into."

My head moved on its own, nodding with excitement, eager to agree. "If they're tired of being mistreated they could—"

"Let me stop you both right there." Regis lifted a hand, cutting us off. "Even if every single one of those ghouls down there decides to revolt, how in the ocean do either of you figure that means they'll help you?"

"If there's one thing I have memorized like the scales on my tailfin it's the look of helplessness," I answered quietly. "My mother may not have taught me the art of magic, but she made sure that look was burned into my memory forever. Defeat and susceptibility go hand in hand, and a rebellion almost always follows if it isn't dealt with. You exploit their vulnerability or you lose your target altogether."

Regis pursed his lips together. "All right, Queen. Since you're suddenly an expert in warfare..."

"I'm not an expert in anything. My mother, however, was a master of deceit and manipulation, and you don't grow up under a shadow like that without learning a thing or two."

"You have my attention. What do you propose?"

"We seize the opportunity. The three of us swim down there and present ourselves as their saviors, as their way out of this unholy existence they call the afterlife."

"You want to offer them that kind of false hope?" Margaret questioned. "After all they've been through already that seems pretty cruel."

"There's nothing false about it. If we defeat Mami Watta, it stands to reason we undo whatever curse she has put them under. If we can get them on our side, our quest becomes that much easier. You're all about infiltration, right Regis? I can guarantee you those things can give us all the inside information you need. Maybe they can even tell us who contacted Margaret about the attack on Finfolkaheem."

"You're basing this all on the assumption that they want a rescuer." Regis paced the ocean floor, swooping his tail out to kick up the sand.

"Why in the ocean would anyone choose to remain a servant of the greatest evil in the ocean?"

"Both of you are forgetting one very important detail: those ghosts are dead. At least here, under Mami Watta, they know what to expect. What happens to them if you do manage to kill their overseer? I don't know about you two, but personally the possibilities of what's next, of what could be waiting on the other side, scares the eels out of me. There's something to be said for knowing your fate instead of having no idea what's coming."

Margaret let out a frustrated puff of bubbles. "So, we're back to no plan."

"No," I insisted. "No, we're not. Regis, I hear you and you make a lot of sense. The evil you know is better than the evil you don't, I get it. But, what other choice do we have here? Look down there. You see how many there are? There's no way we could swim right up to that witch's castle undetected. This is an opportunity we can't afford to pass up. A chance to get inside information, inside help. It's possible to get them on our side."

"You and your possibilities are going to get you killed," Regis grumbled. "So, what then, we just swoop in and announce ourselves to the enemy's muscle?"

Margaret and I smirked at each other, victory once again on our side. "Nothing quite so obvious," I said. "We need to find a way to get one or two of them aside. Get a feel for what kind of chance we have at this working."

"I swear, Fawna, if you get me killed and I come back as one of those things I'm coming after you hard."

"Deal. Let's get moving before we end up having to spend another night here."

Slow and steady, we made our descent into the crevice. The destruction was even more devastating up close. A thick, murky sense of despair polluted the water, the sadness dense enough to suffocate. We realized too late there were no structures left to keep us hidden.

Exposed, Margaret and I followed close behind Regis, holding our breath as we approached the invisible barrier into the forbidden kingdom. The male merrow held a dagger against his tailfin, prepared to strike if need-be. We kept our movements slow, as unthreatening as possible.

"You sure about this?" he asked, trepidation

making his voice unsteady. "We might as well swim into a group of feeding great whites."

I gulped, unable to answer. In truth, I had no idea what we were getting into. We should've spent more time scouting the terrain and less time debating the possibility that we could persuade a pack of ghosts to join our cause. At any rate, suicide mission or not, it was too late to turn back now.

A female apparition glided toward us, the hood of her red and white cloak covering her face. Her long hair floated behind her, tendrils of grey dancing to some inaudible tune. A long, oddly-shaped tail swished behind her, disappearing and reappearing in flashes of static.

Another spirit nearby, this one with no tail at all, turned to observe the newcomers. His face remained like stone, no emotion to be found in his beady black eyes. He darted forward in a dash, flying past the female until he came to a sudden halt mere inches from our faces.

Margaret clutched her brother's shoulder and gasped. Regis threw a protective arm in front of her, the sudden movement startling the ghost as much as me. The thing flinched, but made no sound or further advancements.

"H-hello." I offered a timid smile. "We're not here to make trouble. This is Margaret and Regis. My name is Fawna."

"Don't tell him our names!" Margaret hissed. "Do you know how many spells can be cast just using someone's name?"

The cloaked figure cocked his head at us, blinking as he concentrated on the subtle movements of our lips, as if mesmerized by the sound as we spoke. His mouth twitched, and his jaw opened and closed in a robotic, jerky fashion.

"Can you speak?" I asked, ignoring Margaret's complaint.

Nothing. The departed being stopped his poor attempt at silently mimicking our speech. He swept his gaze across the three of us, but showed no sign of recognizing we were any different than he and the other undead. A school of silverfish swam nearby, the glittering stealing his attention away as suddenly as it was received.

"I don't think he's going to be casting any spells," Regis said. "He couldn't even speak."

Margaret bit her lip and looked around. "I don't like this. For all we know his mind is connected to Mami's."

"It's a little late to worry about that, don't you think? We're here. We might as well have a look around."

"I think we have another visitor." I pointed in the direction of the same undead female who picked up on us from the start.

Slow and steady, she swam up next to us, removing her hood as she came to a stop. Like the one before her, her coal black eyes seemed to stare right past me, into nothing. There was something distinctly different about this woman, though. The ashen, electrified flesh over her heart pulsated with light, a trait not shared by the other ghosts.

The more I studied her features, the more familiar this spirit felt. Too late I realized her tail had a faint blue tint. By the time I recognized the small nose resting on jaggedly sharp cheekbones, Margaret's arms were already stretched wide, prepared to catch my weight as my tail wobbled underneath me.

I fell back, my hand flying over my mouth to cover an involuntary shriek. A tingling numbness traveled up my spine and exploded in my brain. Sparks of light flashed before my eyes, speckling out the figure of the mermaid swimming in front of me.

Regis's shouts barely registered, penetrating my panic as gargled white noise. A heaviness closed around my shoulders and someone shook me, jolting me forward until my head flew back with a loud crack, my ears ringing as the bones in my neck grinded together. The blow released an avalanche of shimmering tears from my eyes.

A deafening high-pitched noise pierced through the water with a razor sharp sting. My chest burned, and I heaved in a gulp of air through my gills. The noise stopped. Only then did I realize the sound came from my own lungs. Saltwater scratched the back of my throat, already hoarse from my blood curdling screams.

"No," I sobbed, no longer caring if Mami Watta or her minions heard me. "No. You can't have her! I won't let you."

The pressure on my hunched over shoulders slid up my neck and cupped my chin. A rough, calloused palm covered my mouth, smothering my cries. Regis turned my face, forcing me to look at him instead of the dead prisoner of the sea witch.

"What in Poseidon is going on?" He spoke to Margaret, not me.

Margaret stuttered, "I... I don't know! She was fine one second, then all the color drained from her face and I thought she was going to faint."

"I'd take fainting over this. At least then she wouldn't lead the enemy straight to us!"

"She's in shock, Regis. Help me get her upright again."

The seafloor shifted as they hoisted me vertical, but Regis kept my line of sight narrow and rigid, fixed on him. "Fawna, can you hear me?"

My lips quivered, and words stuck in my sore throat. I nodded, quick and sharp.

"What happened? What did you see?"

I tried to pull my chin away, to look at the ghostly figure once more, but he still held my chin in place.

"It was the spirit, wasn't it?" Margaret chimed in.

My hands found Regis's forearm and squeezed until he finally let me go. I wiped a lingering shimmer from my eye and glanced at the woman, still loitering in the same spot staring ahead at nothing.

"Who is she, Fawna?" Regis asked gently.

"My mother," I managed. "That's Queen Calypso."

CHAPTER 14

"Queen Calypso." Margaret echoed. "And she's... dead."

"Margaret!" Regis hissed.

"Well, I'm sorry it's just... Well, I think the entire ocean thinks of her as... invincible."

"I used to think so, too," I admitted. "Oh, Mother. What has she done to you?"

I regained myself, swiping the palms of my hands along the front of my tail before inching closer to the thing that was once my mother. Queen Calypso. The most feared being in all the oceans was swimming in front of me, reduced to nothing more than a ghostly aura.

A pang of guilt twisted in my chest. If she wasn't wearing that blasted arm band that kept her from using her magic, she could've fended off Mami Watta without even trying. We condemned her to this fate. By putting that bracelet on her, my sister and I may as well have tied her to an anchor and fed her to the sharks.

"Maybe she's the one who called me," Margaret proposed. "She knew Angelique's wavelength, after all."

Regis snapped his fingers together in front of

Mother's face. When she didn't react, he sneered, "You think this contacted you? I'm not trying to be cruel, but she's just as lost as that other guy who was here. There's nothing going on upstairs. She's got just enough brain activity to keep her useful to Mami Watta. There's no way she would be capable of telepathy right now."

"Could you try?" I asked Margaret. "I was never very good at telepathic communication, even when the other mermaid was expecting my transmission. But maybe you could get through to her. Find out if it was her that sent you the message."

"It's a waste of time." Regis raked his fingers through his hair. "And time is something we don't have a lot of right now."

"We can spare two seconds," Margaret argued. "Besides, she seems to recognize Fawna."

"Because she swam up to us? That other ghost paid us some attention, too."

"But Calypso is still here. Like she's waiting for something. Maybe she's waiting to tell us something. I'm doing this."

Regis threw his hands in the air, once again a begrudgingly accepting defeat. Margaret turned to Mother, watching her for a moment before closing her eyes. A long, taut moment of silence filled the water with a tense energy. A chill enveloped us, as though Margaret pulled the power from the ocean itself to make contact. A faint shade of pink dusted the tops of her green cheeks before she puffed out enough air to blow my hair back.

She opened her eyes, shaking her head. "I'm

sorry, Fawna. All I heard was static."

"It's okay." I cleared my throat. "Thank you for trying."

"Believe it or not, this is actually good news," Regis said.

Margaret patted the small of my back. "Now who's being insensitive?"

"What I mean is, it seems like these apparitions, or whatever, are pretty much unaware. None of them are attacking us, even after the way Fawna screamed bloody fish scales. They're harmless unless Mami Watta orders them otherwise."

"Like puppets," I murmured. "Hollow on the inside. Useless without the puppeteer pulling the strings."

"I don't know what a puppet is, but sure."

"So, you don't think Mami Watta is connected to them?" Margaret asked.

"If she was I think she'd be here by now. This makes our breaking into her castle all the easier. We don't have to fight off an army of the undead to get inside."

"Right." I swished my tail, propelling me forward. "Every castle has a dungeon. Hers is either full of prisoners or her priceless magical relics. Either way, it's a win for us. We should find an entrance from the outside."

"What makes you think there's an outside entrance?"

I arched a challenging brow at him. "I thought you were an expert at infiltration?"

"I am!"

"Every royal, especially a malevolent one, knows how essential a plan B is. You always leave yourself a way out if the obvious route gets cut off. There's a second entrance to her dungeon."

I turned toward the castle, ready to advance when Margaret called to me. "Don't you want to say goodbye?"

Keeping my back to her and the creature of which she spoke, I balled my fists at my side. "To the ghost of who was once my mother? She wouldn't even understand me."

"But maybe you'd feel bet—"

"Let's go," I insisted, and undulated my tail to kick forward.

The merrows caught up quick, swimming by my side when something cold wrapped around my wrist and jerked me back. Startled, I whirled around, and when I saw what now held me captive, I didn't know whether to scream or rejoice.

Mother's fingers, frozen and stinging, clamped down in a hold so fierce the pressure threatened to shatter my bones. I twisted my arm, trying to wiggle free, but her black eyes siphoned me in. The darkness in them swirled, hypnotizing and full of desperation. Even in her death-like state, Mother's power easily overtook my will. Shock seeped into my limbs as whatever spell she cast paralyzed me entirely. As hard as I tried, I couldn't break free of her magical hold.

Margaret's voice echoed somewhere in the distance. "Fawna! She knows it's y—"

Before my merrow companion could finish her

sentence, my eyes rolled in the back of my head. Streaks of color and spots of white flooded my head. An aching started in my skull, but distraction came soon enough.

Shrieks of terror bombarded me from all sides. Cries for mercy and women begging for their lives. The chaos would have been enough to bring me to my knees were I still in my human state, but since I was a mermaid again, all I wanted to do was swim into the deepest darkest cavern I could find. Find a cave so secluded the heartbreaking noise couldn't possibly follow.

I wondered for a brief moment if this was Calypso's punishment; if she was to spend eternity deafened by the tortured bellows of her victims. It seemed fitting, even if she was my mother. Perhaps by drawing me into it, she aimed to trap me in here with her. To force me to suffer, too. As terrifying as the thought was, after what I'd done to Gene, maybe I deserved it just as much as Mother did.

But then, somehow through the countless voices one stood out.

This voice, small and delicate yet full of determination and resistance, didn't scream. Instead, she shouted orders, demanding the others to calm themselves and show pride. To not give the enemy the satisfaction of watching them panic.

Angelique.

I felt her strength just as clearly as I recognized the sound. When I focused harder, I picked up Pauline's frightened chatter. Though I couldn't make out exactly what she said, it was her. This wasn't Mother trying to share her fate with me; she wanted to show me the others were alive!

As if realizing I understood, Mother's binding took another turn. A bright flash of light tore through the pitch black, blasting away the crippling racket. On instinct, my arm flew to shield my eyes from the light, but since the offending illumination was purely in my mind it didn't help. Slowly, the light dimmed. Green spots blotched my vision as I adjusted to my new surroundings.

I looked around, surprised to find myself transported into Mother's hidden chamber beneath her throne. Spell books still piled in the corners, and maps of faraway places plastered the walls. Her cauldron bubbled just in front of me, and my stomach turned at its memory. So much suffering in Atargaris came from the poisons Mother concocted in the black, cast iron pot. As much as Pauline loved books, even she would shudder at the mere sight of the ones in this room. This place still reeked of evil, and the wretched smell filled my mouth with bile.

A flicker on the wall to my right snagged my attention. A sconce on the wall, holding an orb not unlike those created by the merrows, seemed unfamiliar and out of place. I couldn't claim to be that familiar with Mother's secret lair, we weren't permitted to spend much time there considering the magic it housed, but I couldn't recall seeing this particular fixture before. The orb, I knew I never saw. Until I met Margaret, I wasn't even aware of the existence of such a thing.

In my hallucination, I drifted toward the oddity. As I came closer, I realized the beam emanating from the orb shone only up, toward a shelf that held one lone book. Unlike the spell books surrounding me, this one had no writing on the cover at all. An energy came from it, so mysterious and consuming I thought I might burst if I couldn't discover its purpose. I wanted to reach up, to crack the spine and reveal the secrets on the pages, but in this psychic state my movements were at my Mother's mercy.

"Show me, Mother," I requested, the words leaving my physical lips in a soft, respectful plea. "What is it you want me to see?"

A wave crashed into the room, sloshing all Mother's objects and magical relics around. Since I wasn't really there, the force blew past me without effect, but the sheets of the book blew open. Page by page, the parchment flipped, each one without so much as a scribble of ink. I squinted, trying to make sense of the blank book until suddenly, the water became still and the turning stopped.

One final page eared itself over, revealing a hollowed out center. Inside it, a jagged knife with a blackened blade. Most of Mother's weapons were gold, silver, bejeweled—intended to show her status just as much as to inflict fear. She put them on display, a reminder to any of those who might oppose her. But this...

Why would she keep such a plain, worn, and ugly thing? There was something important about this artifact, there had to be.

By Calypso's command, my body turned itself until I faced the maps hanging on the wall. My peripheral vision blurred, until one particular map was all I could see. On it, the Kingdom of the Merrows was an obvious landmark, with a dotted trail leading to a circled X. Scrawled beneath it, in a rusted substance I was almost certain was blood, the word *Watta*.

Goosebumps covered my real flesh, and I shuddered at the chilliness encircling me. A new voice crept into my brain, one I knew and feared like nothing else in the ocean. My mother's voice, commanding yet crackling. To communicate was a struggle, but, like the stubborn royal she was, Calypso found a way.

"Get the blade." Her whisper bounced off the walls of her imaginary lair, slamming into me with a commanding force.

"What good will it do?" I asked, my voice shaking. It didn't make any sense. What power could such a humble weapon have over a being as powerful as Mami Watta? She was immortal, immune to earthly threats.

Mother repeated her order. "Get the blade and kill Mami Watta."

The scene around me vanished, a blast of cold assaulting my senses the second her voice ceased. Oxygen flew from my lungs. Dizzy and disoriented, I rubbed my eyes and straightened my tail, refusing to topple over like a weakling once again. I reached out for Mother, the dead version of her, and she held me steady while I regained myself.

Panting, I used my free hand to clutch at my heart, willing its beat to regain its normal rhythm.

Victory required a calm mind, and a calm mind required steady wits. Moments ago, I was unsure victory could even be had, and now it was all but certain.

We could win this.

Mother had faith in me, so much so that she fought the grip of death itself to reveal her most devastating weapon. And if a ruler as experienced and terribly successful as Queen Calypso believed in me, who was I to disagree?

Things were different now. No longer would I succumb to my own panic and fear of the unknown. A confident smirk played on my lips as I looked over at the merrows, who watched me as if they expected me to break down again.

Not this time. Thanks to Queen Calypso, we had a plan.

CHAPTER 15

"**W**hat the starfish just happened, Fawna?" Margaret pried me from the grip of my undead mother, watching her close with fear etched in the wrinkles near her eyes.

The late queen's figure slowly turned to fog, dissipating in the water until she was gone. A sense of loss squeezed at my chest as I watched her vanish, but I shook it off and returned my attention to the battle at hand. There would be time to mourn her later, I decided.

"A vision." I nodded toward Mami Watta's castle. "She showed me how we're going to take down that sea witch."

Regis rested a careful hand on my shoulder, as if he thought I might crumble if he wasn't careful. "I know she's your mother, but do you really think we can trust her? I mean, she was almost as evil as the creature we're after."

"Of course we can trust her," I spat.

Margaret lifted an unsure shoulder. "I don't know. Why would she help us? It's possible she was under Mami Watta's spell and just showed you what—"

"Think of it this way," I started, "Calypso wants

revenge. Mami killed her, so naturally she'd do anything she could to make sure her assassination is avenged. Queen Calypso can't be controlled. Not by King Odom, not by Mami Watta. That's why they both did their best to take her out of the equation altogether."

Regis shifted in place. He looked at me, brows furrowed. "If she's still conscious enough to have such a strong hold on wanting revenge, what's that say about the others? Is Calypso special or do the others still carry around an agenda, too?"

"Oh." Margaret's mouth turned downward as she scanned the seemingly endless sea of undead who still paced around Mami Watta's palace. "That's a dreadful thought; to be just aware enough to remember it all but too dead to do anything other than what some nasty old sea witch tells you."

I couldn't dwell on it, not right now. "All the more reason to keep pressing forward."

"Agreed. What did she show you? Where do we go now?"

"We need to find a way to Atargatis. Swimming there would take weeks if not months. I don't suppose either of you can create a tunnel the way a fin-man can?"

Margaret's shoulders slumped. "I'm afraid not. The merrows aren't gifted with the ability to manipulate water. That gift is only for the Finfolk to have. Much like mermaids and your song."

"Looks like we're making a pitstop then."

"*Pitstop*?" Regis repeated.

"We need to find a fin-man."

"You mean swim all the way back to Finfolka-heem? Even if we could make it in time there's no telling if any of them are left alive."

"Awake," Margaret corrected. "The woman that contacted me told me they were asleep, Regis. Not dead. She was very clear on that point."

"We're welcome from my mother, by the way. She spoke to me, too. And I have no intention of returning to Finfolkaheem. Mami's spell has worn off. They're awake, I heard them, but they're not back there."

"Where are they, then?"

I swiveled my tail, turning to face the enemy's lair head-on. "Right under our noses."

"Fantastic," Regis grunted sarcastically. "Back to sneaking in through the dungeon, I take it? Let's get on with it then. We're running out of moonlight."

Careful not to further disturb the wandering puppets of death, we made our way to the back of the castle. It almost seemed too easy; no walls or security around the entire perimeter. Then again, most intelligent beings wouldn't dare try getting past her minions. The sight of them alone would be enough to ward them off. Mami relied on them too much, and just maybe that would be her weakness in the end.

Ordinary cement blocks from the human world formed a sturdy structure that housed the great sea witch. The castle resembled those I saw on television, impossibly high and unnecessarily extravagant. Even a gargoyle of sorts perched menacingly at its doorstep, though the thing appeared more like a mutant octopus than a winged demon. No stained windows graced the smooth stone surface, ensuring Mami Watta complete privacy to conduct her treacherous deeds.

"Strangely human design," I wondered, mostly to myself. "Where could she have gotten these materials?"

Regis just shrugged, not nearly as impressed as I was at the connection between worlds. "She's had those poor ghosts pedaling their goods on land during the full moons, remember? I'm sure they were able to pick up whatever resources she required in the process."

"Look there!" Margaret pointed at the base of the castle, where the tiniest hint of an iron door remained unburied. "I bet that's a way in."

"I never doubted you." Regis gave me a smug grin before swiping his tail back and forth, dusting away the sand layer by layer until the rest of the door showed itself. "It's pretty small, but I bet we can squeeze through."

A heavy iron handle, nearly rusted in place, was the last thing between us and Mami's domain. I held my breath as Regis yanked on it, peeling the door open with a loud creak. Complete and absolute darkness waited for us on the other side. The merrow peeked his head inside, then twirled his finger until an orb formed at its tip.

"What's the human expression? Ladies first."

Margaret rolled her eyes and shoved him aside, manifesting her own ball of light. I followed close on her tail. Regis closed the door behind us, and I winced as the old bolts clattered in dissent.

A nauseating musky odor surrounded us now that we were closed in. The merrows held up their light sources, revealing a narrow corridor with green mildewed walls. The occasional smudge of rusted red, blood without a doubt, made the blood in my veins freeze. This place and the malevolence it held made Mother's secret throne room feel like a church.

"She needs to unleash a swarm of suckerfish down here." I pinched my nose and prayed my gills wouldn't stop taking in air in protest.

Margaret held a silencing hand at the same moment Regis's fingers dug into my shoulders, yanking me back to stop. "Did you hear that?" she asked.

The soft ripple of disturbed water bumped into my back as Regis nodded. I closed my eyes, trying to find the slightest sound. "I don't hear anything."

As soon as I said the words, a small blast of bubbles shot out from an intersecting hallway. Every instinct I had told me to turn tail and swim. Swim back to the safety of the open ocean and keep swimming until I was out of danger's reach, but my tail anchored itself in place. I hadn't come this far just to stop now.

In a rush, the three of us bolted toward the passageway. We careened around the corner and down another corridor, the end of which opened into a wide open room. Somehow in the pandemonium, I wound up in front of Margaret, and just as we rushed into the new space I collided with a hard body. Tail over head, I toppled back, landing hard on my elbows.

"Fawna!" Margaret screeched as she helped me sit up.

"I'm all right," I insisted. "What was—"

"Fawna?" A foreign male's voice echoed in the empty space.

Regis threw himself in front of us, his shoulders back and knife out, ready to strike. "Who are you?"

I sought out the newcomer, first finding a pair of two legs covered in shark skin pants planted firmly on the sea floor. His torso shimmered, almost glowing. A fin-man, I realized when I saw no gills on his neck. He dragged his knuckles over his thick, fiery red beard before holding his arms up defensively.

"Do you think he's one of them?" Regis asked. "One of Mami's minions?"

I shook my head and tugged down on Regis's arm, urging him to lower the weapon, but he resisted. "No. His eyes, look at them. They're still green, not beady like the others."

"That doesn't mean he isn't working for her. Just because he isn't dead doesn't mean he's on our side."

"Margaret," the stranger took a tentative step forward, "it's me! For the ocean's sake, it hasn't been that long."

The female merrow lifted her orb, shaking as she inched toward the fin-man. "Lennox." She gasped. "Regis, put that thing down! This is King Lennox, Angelique's husband."

Regis tightened his jaw before obliging, lowering his blade just enough to satisfy his sister. "What's the King of Finfoklaheem doing in these waters?"

"Same thing as my wife's sister, I suspect." Lennox looked at me, a kin-like familiarity in his eyes. "Finally I meet my sister-in-law. I'm just sorry it's under these circumstances."

I smiled politely and said, "I don't understand. When I spoke to Angelique she said you were on an expedition."

"A hunt. I was off the coast of Maine, actually. The lobster there is a great improvement on the still tainted fish in our kingdom. But the ocean, she called me back. Something shifted in her water, I could feel it. I swam home as fast as I could but..."

"What's the condition of Finfolkaheem?" Margaret asked gently. "Was the damage great?"

"I arrived just as most of my people were waking up from some kind of spell. They told me a sudden rush of foggy water overcame the kingdom, swallowing the palace whole. The sleep came instantly. I knew it had to be Mami Watta's black magic. No one, save Calypso, would be capable of debilitating an entire kingdom at once! When I couldn't find Angelique I struck up a tunnel to bring me here."

"She's here," I interjected. "I can feel it. Her and Pauline both. And my Randy."

"I told Angelique the first time we came here to keep her distance from that sea witch."

"Do you have any idea where she and the others might be?" Regis asked. "Maybe we can manage to get them out before we make our way to Atargatis."

Lennox tapped his chin again, eyeing the merrow with skepticism written all over his face. "Strange to see a merrow involved in this quarrel. Margaret I understand. She and Angelique went through a lot together. Last I heard, though, your clan wasn't quite ready to make allies with us Finfolk."

"King Lennox, I think I speak for all the merrows when I say we'll side with just about anybody when the common foe is Mami."

Margaret let out a sarcastic laugh. "Don't let him fool you. It took more than a little persuasion to enlist his help. We're acting on our own. Our clan has no knowledge of the threat at hand and it would probably be wise to keep it that way."

"Why do you say that?" Lennox scoffed. "If they knew maybe we wouldn't have to fight this battle alone. Your clan is responsible for keeping the magic of the ocean in check. We could use their help."

"I don't think we could convince the majority to stand against her. As powerful as we are, we play by certain rules. Mami Watta has no rules, no boundaries. She'll do whatever it takes to win."

"That's what you're supposed to do! You fight to win, not to lose. There's more at stake here than the integrity of the merrows. Sometimes rules must be bent to ensure the right side is victorious."

Regis finally stuck his knife back into its sheath before crossing his arms in front of his chest. "We understand that is the Finfolk way. You battle for your own cause in whatever way you see fit without apology. That method, however, does not suit the merrows. We won't shy away from the light."

"Then you will lose," Lennox said through gritted teeth.

An image of the blackened blade hanging on the wall beneath Mother's throne flashed in my mind.

If it was powerful enough to defeat the sorceress of darkness herself, it no doubt came from the darkness itself. If I used it, it would mean wading in the world where evil was born. I risked sacrificing whatever soul I had left in doing so.

It hardly mattered. My mind was made up. I would do whatever it took to save my family and the entire ocean from the evil that already lurked beneath its surface. I would use black magic, bathe in it if I had to, if it meant my sisters and my child were safe again.

"Fawna." Regis's stern call pulled me from my thoughts. "I said, where do you stand on this?"

I moved my gaze between the merrows and the fin-man, perfectly aware for the first time of my place in this world. The merrows lived and breathed ideology, while finfolk craved adventure and the beat of the war drum. Atargatis belonged somewhere in the middle. My sisters and I worked to close the rivalry between humans and mermaids. Angelique ended the conflict that started with King Odom. We were the peacekeepers between worlds, and now it was my turn to restore balance.

"I'll do what needs to be done," I told them all. "When the time comes, I'll use whatever magic, light or dark, that is needed. The integrity of the merrows will never come into question, you have my word. I will take the blame for whatever forces need to be called upon."

"You must be joking," Regis grumbled.

Margaret shushed her brother before adding, "Fawna, you're better than this!"

"No, I'm not," I proclaimed without a hint of shame. "You are. The both of you. But the things I've done in the past makes taking out this monster seem like an angelic act. After all, is wielding the darkness to remove a villain really an act of evil? I don't think so. At any rate, it's my soul that's up for judgment, not yours. I'll take the risk. We're running out of time. Lennox, do you know where my sisters are?"

"Thank the sea one of you has enough sense to see the truth." Lennox jerked his head toward the vacant room. "I sensed some disruption in the water this way."

CHAPTER 16

"Stop swimming!" Margaret's sudden outburst startled us to a halt.

We snaked through a few more corridors like disoriented eels, but the maze-like design of Mami Watta's palace kept us from locating the prisoners. Every time Lennox would claim we were closing in on the sizeable disturbance he sensed, the hall we swam in came to a dead end. We just barely turned around and headed for another route when Margaret stopped us.

"What is it?" I asked, trying to read her face in the flickers of light cast off by her orb.

"It's Angelique. I just heard her."

Regis looked at Lennox, then me, and we all shrugged. "I didn't hear anything," he said.

"Neither did I," the fin-man agreed.

Margaret waved her arms around in a frantic, frustrated sweep. "Not out here!" She brought a pointed index finger to her temple. "In here. I've been trying to contact her telepathically since we got here. Up until now I haven't heard a thing but..."

"She reached out to you?" I asked, hopeful. "Tell us what you heard."

"I... I'm not sure. I couldn't make it out. Her

voice was coming in and out, flickering. That's why I stopped so suddenly; I thought if I stayed in one spot it might come in clearer."

"Try again," Lennox urged.

"I am trying!" Tears brimmed in her eyes, but without the same shimmer as a mermaid's. They were washed away by the surrounding water almost as soon as they appeared. "It's just silence."

I tugged on a strand of my white hair, twisting it around my finger to help me concentrate. "She's in a dead zone."

"She's not dead!"

"No, no. A dead zone is... well, on land we have these devices called cell phones. We use them to talk to one another from long distances, sort of like your telepathy only technology based. Every once in a while though, you mysteriously end up in one particular spot that never seems to have any signal. You can't make a call or send a text, but just a few feet in either direction and boom! You're back in business."

Margaret blinked at me. "I didn't understand half of what you just said, but I think I got the basic idea. You're saying Angelique can't reach out because where she's being held there's some sort of invisible barrier."

"Right. I'm sure Mami put it there to keep her from giving away any information she may have gathered just by being... well, Angelique."

"Then we break the barrier," Lennox said matter-of-factly.

Regis chuckled, his annoyance more than obvious. "Not every problem can be solved by hitting things."

"It's not a literal barrier," I explained. "Regis is right, we can't just smash it. There's probably an incantation or something that could tear it apart, but I haven't the slightest idea how a spell like that would work."

Lennox held a hand out to Margaret. "What about you, Margaret?"

"Sure, but it takes more than just words," she clarified. "We'd need a number of things, including an item belonging to Angelique."

The fin-man removed a necklace and shoved it at her. "Here, she gave me this."

"It's not enough, Lennox. I'm sorry. Everything else I need I have, just not here. But, the good news is if she's fighting past whatever interference has been put up then she has to be close."

"She's right," said a menacing, raspy voice from behind.

All three of us whirled around, immediately alerted to the intruder. Margaret and Regis floated behind us with their orbs, but the light they let off couldn't reach deep enough into the corridor to show the face of the woman speaking.

On the wall to our right, her shadow stretched to the very top, the shape of it cut off and contorted onto the flat ceiling. The lightshow revealed something on her shoulders slithering, and a quick forked tongue darted out and back in its mouth.

A snake. I recalled Gilcrest's vision back in Finfolkaheem. He spoke of snakes, and Angelique immediately connected it to the enemy.

"Admiring Rellik, I see," she snickered. "Angelique found him fascinating the first time they met, too."

"Revolting is probably a more accurate word," I spat at her, wishing my words would strike her with the venom of the hideous creature she carried around like a fear-inducing trophy.

She threw her head back and cackled. "He's a ball python, dear. He doesn't have venom."

"How... how did you—"

"No, he doesn't take the easy approach to his attack. Any weak creature can use poison. He finds it far more entertaining to lie in wait until his victim suspects him the least. Then, and only then, my dear Princess, does he strike. Do you know what he does next?"

I didn't want to play this game. Squaring my shoulders I said, "Since you killed my mother you may address me as Queen, not Princess."

"Do you know what he does next, Queen Fawna? He coils himself around the poor unfortunate who got in his way and squeezes the life out of her until every last bit of life that once shined so bright in her eyes disappears entirely."

"Quite the informative lecture, Sorceress. But, what happens when the prey bites back?"

"Then she starts a war she doesn't know how to finish, putting everyone else in the path of the snake's wrath. I told you that though, didn't I? I made myself clear when I met you inside your cozy little land dwelling what would happen if you returned to the sea."

"You knew I couldn't let you get away with this. That I couldn't just let you steal my baby away and pretend it never happened. What kind of person would that make me?"

She swished forward with a subtle grace, her cocoa skin now recognizable. I took in the sight of the countless lines tattooed along her arms and chest, all the way up her neck until the wrinkles on her face took up their path. Deceivingly friendly eyes twinkled back at me, perfectly suited to the grandmother-like face they were set upon.

"I hate to be the one to remind you, dear, but you're not a person. You've spent more time among them than any being of the sea should, so the lapse in memory is understandable. You're a mermaid. Not just any mermaid, no. The heir to the throne of Atargatis. The descendant of the most vicious ruler the ocean has ever known. Our world is filled with things better left behind, spawn. Your bloodline is one of them."

"You're lying," Regis exclaimed. "You're not trying to exterminate their bloodline, you're trying to use it."

"My quarrel isn't you with you and your kind, Merrow. Swim away now and I'll forget your involvement in this offense."

"We can't do that." Margaret's voice strained under her fear, but she held her ground. "You're too powerful, Mami Watta. You know it's our duty to oversee the balance of magic in the ocean. We can't allow you to get any stronger, and if you go through with this..."

A flash of rage flashed across Mami Watta's face, washing away the matronly façade. "And who's going to stop me? This little trout's mother couldn't hold her own against me. What in the ocean makes you think she can do what Calypso couldn't?"

I tried to rush forward, but Margaret and Regis held me back by the arms. The urge to wrap my fingers around her throat and make her choke on my mother's name burned me from the inside, cauterizing my senses. As I jolted forward, a sharp pain radiated through my shoulders. Despite being almost certain my arm was dislocated, I kept lunging at her like a wild beast.

"The only reason Calypso couldn't take you out is because of that stupid bracelet! It kept her magic stunted. She couldn't fight back, and you used that weakness like a coward."

"That's right, the bracelet you put on her was her downfall. You made her weak so you wouldn't have to contend with her. Your sisters and you are the cause of everything that's about to come. Remember that in your afterlife, won't you? This is your fault."

I settled, letting her words seep into me like acid. She was right. One way or another, an evil was going to rain fire on our underwater world. Be it my mother, King Odom, Mami Watta... there was no telling how many other villains sat in wait for their turn to strike out.

At least Calypso kept her reign contained within our kingdom. She didn't spread the misery, forcing every other clan in the ocean to suffer because of her pain. None of the others showed themselves simply because they feared facing my mother, and now, because my sisters and I squelched that deterrent we unwittingly unleashed an avalanche of evil.

Lennox squeezed my shoulder, rocking me slightly to pull my attention to him. "Don't listen to her. She's trying to get into your mind, to twist things, to separate you from what we've come here to do. Don't let her spin your mind into a tunnel of nonsense."

I squinted at him, trying to figure out why his inflection came out so disjointed.

"Ah, Lennox." Mami moved her attention to the fin-man. "You've returned to my waters. I'm surprised after what happened the last time I saw you. I let you go then, fin-man. I won't make the same mistake twice."

Lennox tossed her a condescending laugh. "I wasn't afraid of you then and I'm not now, sea witch."

The muscles in his arm rippled and rolled, the movement ever so slight yet constant. He held his hand behind his back at a strange angle as he spoke.

"Oh, you are most definitely frightened now. The difference is this time instead of using fancy words and false promises to woo your little mermaid into joining my conquest, I'm swimming over here trying to think of the fun ways I can torture her for turning me down. You may not value your own life, but Angelique's is priceless. Young love. The ultimate weakness, don't you agree?"

We held a collective breath, waiting for Lennox to lose his temper. Instead, he closed his eyes and took a deep breath in an uncharacteristic attempt to calm himself. When he opened them again, he again squeezed my shoulder with the hand not out of the sea witch's sight. I flitted my gaze behind him, just quick enough to keep Mami from noticing.

A tiny whirlpool started at his fingertips. The fin-man drew a tunnel in the water, the start of an escape route. The vortex grew slow but steady while Mami watched Lennox, growing suspicious every second as she waited for his response.

I jumped in, offering a meager distraction while Lennox got a hold on his formation. *Keep her talking.* "You lay a scale on either of my sisters and I swear I'll—"

"You'll what, my dear?" Mami challenged. "I don't think you realize what kind of predicament you've gotten yourself into. You're cornered, trapped like a baby seal in the middle of a pod of killer whales. By following your sister here you took the bait I set out for you. With you and your entire family out of the way, I can and will finish what I started. I won't just rule the ocean. Thanks to the blood flowing in your child's veins, I'll dominate land and sea."

"You won't kill Sebastian. I won't let you hurt him!"

"But, Queen Fawna," she cooed and stuck out her bottom lip, as if coddling an infant, "you'll be dead. Every single one of you will be dead."

Before I could respond, Lennox stepped in front of me, releasing his creation. "You'll have to kill me first."

Wind from the spiraling water whipped my hair across my face, but not before I caught a satisfying glimpse of Mami Watta's wide eyes. A suction started in the corridor, pulling those of us who were close enough toward the transportation tunnel.

"Go!" Lennox yelled over Mami's indecipherable protests.

Regis and Margaret wasted no time leaping in headfirst. I held out my hand for the fin-man, but he swatted it away.

"Get in before it closes. It'll take you where you need to go."

My tail threatened to sweep out from under me, but I clenched my torso to keep from getting pulled in. "Not without you!"

He rounded a ball of water in his hand, launching it at the sea witch with enough force to crack the wall it collided with. "I have to hold her off as long as I can. Get what you need! A friend of mine is there, Ainsley. He'll help you get back when you're ready."

I hovered frozen between him and the only way out. My conscience ate at my heart, torn between swimming and fighting. This fin-man loved my sister with such a fierce loyalty he was willing to sacrifice himself to save her. Somewhere in this castle my Randy sat alone and afraid. Sebastian was here, no doubt just as confused by this dark new world, terrified and feeling abandoned.

How could I leave them again when I was so close?

"Fawna!" Lennox hurled another water bomb, hitting Mami Watta so hard she flew back into the wall. "You can't save anybody without that relic your mother showed you. Get it, then come back and finish this."

CHAPTER 17

Most humans believe in a heaven, or something like it. Some cosmic refuge one's soul seeks for safe haven once they've left this life. Randy once told me he imagined it to be a place of complete peace and overwhelming calm. A state of total bliss and relaxation. Maybe it's because I lived most of my life in chaos, but a place so quiet seemed more like a punishment than a reward.

For me, in my mind, the ideal heaven was more like Lennox's tunnel. Roaring and full of thrill, with white noise whizzing by your ears every second, forcing you to shut everything else out. Inside this raging tide, I was indestructible. The creatures of the ocean, both innocent and terrible, may as well have been as fixed as the ocean floor for as fast as I careened by them. They couldn't get me here.

My responsibilities couldn't reach me here.

I couldn't decide why this tunnel felt so much different than the one created by Gilcrest. This time, there was no motion sickness or disorientation. Perhaps there was something different about its make-up since Gilcrest was only half fin-man. Maybe it was because I knew what to expect when I leaped in this time. Probably, it was because I had changed so much since then that the idea of a little fast water didn't seem so terrifying anymore.

Either way, I wouldn't dwell on it. I laid my head back and closed my eyes, enjoying the rush that tingled from the tip of my tail through my entire body. Butterflies danced in my stomach, and I soaked in every second that I could shut it all out. All the screams, the expectations, the weight of everything I'd lost and everything I still stood to lose.

In that moment, they faded in the distance. I dozed off, content and for the first time I could remember, without fear that my happiness would come crashing down around me.

I suppose that's why I was uncharacteristically unprepared when it did.

My body sensed the danger for me, jolting me awake. The next thing I knew I was airborne, slicing through the water like an anchor seeking the sand. Head over tail I rolled forward, the sea doing little to slow my departure as Lennox's tunnel collapsed around me. *I should've paid attention*, I chastised myself. At least in my discomfort the last time I swam through one of these vortexes I had good sense to notice the end before I went through it!

Now, without preparing for the sudden change in speed, I barreled toward the ground. Dizzy and still spinning, my mind didn't register what the colorful anomaly in my path was. Almost the instant I realized it was there at all, I crashed into it, and a searing pain scraped up my face and across my torso, so terrible I couldn't even scream before everything went dark.

A mess of merciful red tangles draped around me, blocking out any trace of light. My blurry vision struggled to focus, but after a few blinks I could at least make out the outline of a feminine face. Until something pressed against my forehead and I closed my eyes again to cry out in agony.

Someone shushed me, then brushed aside a strand of my hair. "I know it hurts," a familiar voice cooed, "but I have to clean out the bits of sand or your skin will just scar over them."

"Eileen?" I croaked, swallowing hard against the burn in my throat. Saltwater was a fantastic cleaning agent, but it did little to ease the pain of open wounds.

"You've been in your human form a long time. Your body isn't as resilient as it used to be. The damage will heal, just don't expect any miraculous timing."

"I guess our body adapted to the constant danger down here." I sat up and looked around, surprised to find myself in my mother's old sleeping quarters. Well, more recently Aunt Myrtle's.

Eileen leaned back, scrutinizing my face. She pursed her lips and sighed. "Such a pretty face, too."

"That bad, is it?"

"You'll survive, at least. You probably shouldn't get up just yet, though. You had a pretty nasty concussion. Let yourself rest."

"Regis and Margaret..."

"Are in much better condition than you are. They came through that tunnel like they'd done it a hundred times. We saw you fly through the end of it with about as much grace as a jellyfish in a hurricane."

Heat burned my face, lighting up every cut. "I like to make an entrance," I joked.

"You certainly did that!" Eileen laughed, then took my hand in hers to hold with affection. "We've missed you, Fawna. It's wonderful to have you back."

"It's nice to be home," I admitted.

"The council is eager to meet with you. Those of us still alive, that is."

I stretched my neck, noting how heavy it felt again. My break was over. "How many did we lose?"

"Too many. There are maybe a dozen merfolk left here. A few took sanctuary in Atlantis, but most preferred to stay and rebuild."

"Rebuild with *what*? They had no leader, no guidance. No magic."

"Not to sound conceited, but the Atlantians were generous. They sent over supplies and citizens to help. It's taken some hard work and the days have been long, but we've managed to at least begin the process of starting over."

"Again," I added bitterly. "These poor people. It seems like every time they get a few stones in place some new evil force comes along and wipes out all their progress."

"It's disheartening to say the least."

"I don't know why they don't all just abandon me to the wreckage. They deserve some peace. Maybe I should send them to Atlantis to find some."

"We would take them in without hesitation, Queen, but I wouldn't be so hasty. These merfolk are here because they want to be. Because they knew you would come back. They stayed loyal to you, Your Majesty."

I shifted under the title, instantly uncomfortable and out of place. The crown wasn't even on my head yet, and I was already sinking under its weight. These merfolk deserved a confident, worthy ruler.

They deserved Aunt Myrtle.

A lump formed in my throat at her memory. It wasn't so long ago she slept on this very bed rock. She sat on the same throne that waited for me and rebuilt this same kingdom from rubble. How in the ocean could I even begin to compare to her?

I couldn't. It was as simple as that. But, I could be there for my people the way they have been here for me, waiting and accepting. This whole ordeal wasn't just about me and my Sebastian and my sisters. The safety of every mermaid in my kingdom was my responsibility. I had to eliminate the threat once and for all.

"Have Regis and Margaret filled you in on our situation?" I lifted my shaking chin, trying my best to appear ready and poised.

"They have indeed. I find the whole thing curious to say the least."

"What's so curious about a sea witch causing mayhem around here? It seems that such an occurrence should be considered normal in Atargatis by now."

Eileen laughed, the tension releasing from her

shoulders. "What I mean is, Lennox and Angelique left here looking for Mami Watta. Before they came to rule Finfolkaheem, that is. It was just after we defeated King Odom and his army. Long before this mess started."

"What are you talking about? I only just left Lennox and I spoke to Angelique just over a week ago. Neither of them said anything about searching her out."

"It's true. I heard Angelique left Lennox in Finfolkaheem because fin-men are forbidden from entering Mami's waters. She sought her out, tried to get her to help heal your mother."

"Maybe Angelique didn't get that far. It's possible she decided to stay in Finfolkaheem when she realized they were going to elect Lennox as king."

"That's certainly possible, yes. I suppose that's a question for Angelique when we get her home."

"Agreed."

"Now, rest up. The council does want to discuss our strategy but I told them not until you're in proper condition to do so."

"I appreciate your concern, Eileen, but I'm ready to get to work." As I tried to swim up, she closed her grip on my shoulders and forced me back down.

Eileen shook her head. "I know you're anxious to get them back but please, you've got to recover first or you're no good to any of us."

"My people have been out there rebuilding this kingdom stone by stone. You can't ask me to stay in bed while they continue to do so. Besides, I don't have time to recover. Mami Watta isn't going to postpone her ceremony just because I hit my head."

"Just as stubborn as your mother. All right, Queen Fawna, I'll send for the others. In the meantime, what do you say we have a look around? See what you're fighting for."

"I know all too well what I'm fighting for, but I'd love to see the merfolk that stayed behind. I'd like to express my gratitude for their loyalty to my family."

Eileen smiled wide, the dimples in her cheeks nearly reaching her eyes. "I think that's a fabulous idea."

As we swam through what was left of my home, my heart ached. Whatever attack Mami sent to us was far worse than what she sent to Finfolkaheem. Rubble littered the seafloor, though the huge piles of broken stone and chipped seashell revealed just how much the Atlantians and merfolk had already cleaned up.

Looking around, it appeared the humans sent down one of their bombs to wipe us out. Nearly all the grottos caved in, leaving little room for the merfolk to live. Inside, the castle gave no indication as to the damage to the outside, mostly to the upper levels. A pile of busted coral sat on top of where the school used to be.

The cargo ship where Mother held our festivities was in the distance, but even from here I could see it was blown to bits.

"Good Poseidon." I covered my mouth, swallowing bile. "I should've been here."

"If you'd have been here we might have lost you as well. Then where would your people be? With you alive, you offer the one thing these merfolk need the most. Hope."

Whether she was right or not, the guilt still nipped at my tail. Had I been here instead of soaking up the sun in a world where I didn't really belong... well, maybe one more mermaid carrying a spear could've made some kind of impact.

I tucked my regret away, determined to forget what I couldn't take back. "Where have these mermaids been sleeping?"

Eileen answered, "Inside the castle. It's the only habitable place left, I hope you don't mind."

"Of course I don't. Give them whatever supplies they require. Food from our kitchen if there's any left. Whatever we have, it's theirs now."

"I think perhaps we should meet with the council before we start granting such liberties."

I stopped short and spun around. "Eileen, please don't misunderstand. I'm grateful beyond words for everything you and the Atlantians have done for my people, but the council is hereby dissolved."

The red-headed mermaid's eyes opened wide. "But, Queen Fawna—"

"We have less than a dozen citizens left. We don't have a clan anymore, what we have is a family. Every member of this family is entitled to be heard. Right now we need ideas. Some fantastic concept to save us. We can't afford to limit ourselves to the opinions of just a few, not right now."

"Fawna?" A female's voice came from behind, full of surprise and shaky optimism. "Queen Fawna, is that you?"

I took a deep breath before I turned to face the first expecting face of many. Ms. Star, a mermaid who served as our clan's powers teacher for many, many, years, approached fast with her arms stretched wide. Welcoming her in, I held her head against my chest as she sobbed into me.

"Ms. Star, I'm so happy to see you're all right."

The mermaid who spent countless hours teaching me about our abilities and our culture peered up at me, shimmering tears staining her face. I swallowed hard, willing away the tightness in my chest. If I hoped to lead any of them I couldn't show weakness. They needed to at least believe I knew what I was doing.

"I'm a little worse for wear," she admitted. "We all are. But, we're alive. Oh, I knew you'd come back. I told them all you would."

"Of course I came back. How could I not knowing the state of Atargatis?"

"Some of the merfolk thought you might stay ashore. That you'd made a new life for yourself."

Her words made me think of Randy and the life I planned to create with him. Once upon a time part of me did hope that one day we could get married and buy a cute little house just close enough to the sea to remind me of where I came from. Then, recalling the night he actually did propose and as the possibility came within my grasp I found myself sick at the prospect.

My time back in the ocean, though chaotic to say the least, made me realize it wasn't Randy I was doubtful of. It was land. Deep inside I knew I didn't belong there, that this was my home. I had to choose between my kingdom and Randy, and looking at Ms. Star now I knew the choice wasn't mine. It had been made for me. These people needed me far more than Randy would once I got him out of that sea witch's clutches.

"Atargatis is my home," I assured her. "And I won't leave it or you to the sea's mercy. Gather the others. I have news to tell."

CHAPTER 18

The picture of lonely. That's the best way I could describe how my mother's old throne looked from across the room. The solid gold seat sparkled, winking at me with its shine. Priceless emeralds and rubies lined the rim of the back and the sides of the arm rest. On the table next to it, the diamond crown that would tie me to it and this kingdom forever.

With shaking hands, my tail dragged me over to the antique chair fit only for a royal. I brushed the sharp tip of the crown with my finger tip, but decided against putting it on. The last time I wore a tiara was when I was a princess training to rule under my mother.

I knew then I would be queen one day. As the oldest, the expectation had been there since birth. Then one day in her anger, Mother pronounced the honor to be Angelique's, and from that moment on, I never thought about the notion again. Now I hovered, once again faced with the burden. It seemed destiny was an inescapable authority.

I shook the quiver out of my limbs and turned around to sit, the cold metal singeing the bare skin on my back. Instinctively my muscles tightened, arching me away from the discomfort, but I forced myself to ease into it. From this vantage point, I could see the entire throne room without trying. There wasn't a single crevice out of sight. So when a strange fin-man walked in, I had no trouble at all spotting him.

"You look really uncomfortable," he noted with a smirk.

"I am. I'm sorry, I didn't see you at the assembly. You are?"

"Ainsley. I was there; I just hung back a bit. I'm not an Atlantian or Atargatian so I didn't want to chime in."

"You're Lennox's friend. He told me you'd be here."

"Glad to hear he still remembers an old friend. You did great out there, by the way. That speech was quite inspirational with all your talk about everyone having a voice now. Pretty moving stuff."

I leaned forward, trying to read into this blond fin-man. He was either being casually sincere or brutally sarcastic. Unable to determine which, I responded with a drawn out, "Thank you."

"There's more to what you told them, though, isn't there?"

"I beg your pardon?"

He held up his arms. "I just mean after you said that sea witch has Angelique and Pauline and the others you said you knew how to stop her. You cut that part pretty short, didn't really explain how. I figure there must be a good explanation for you leaving that part out."

"You figure correctly, Ainsley." I arched a brow at him, a warning to watch his step. "Tell me, you said you don't consider yourself a citizen of Atargatis. Why is it you're here then?"

"I think you and I find ourselves, as the humans like to say, in the same boat."

"And what brings you to that conclusion?"

"Your human boyfriend is in danger and the sea witch has Jewel, too. I'll do whatever it takes to get her back just the same as you're willing to do for him."

"Oh." I cleared my throat. "That's right. I remember Jewel swimming off to find you when we first arrived in Finfolkaheem. Angelique said you were quite worried about her."

"Quite worried," he parroted. "You could say that. I told Jewel a hundred times she should stay with us. That our kingdom was better prepared and protected. No offense, but we have a pretty big army."

"So I've heard. You were there, then, when the fog descended on your kingdom?"

He nodded, quick and to the point. "I was. Jewel was talking to your human friend when I stepped out of the room for just a minute to get something to eat. Next thing you know I'm waking up on the floor and the whole bunch are gone."

"What did all your preparations do for you then?"

The fin-man stumbled on his words, taken aback by my point. "There's no way anyone could have prepared for that!"

"Exactly. It doesn't matter what clan she takes residency with, as long as Mami Watta and creatures like her roam the sea there's no such thing as 'safe'."

"All right." He puffed out his chest then crossed his arms in front of himself. "Let's start with Mami before we go after the whole ocean."

"Probably wise," I agreed, my tone just as clipped as his. "Imagine, if you will, a potion so powerful it could kill even the immortal with just a single prick of the skin. All that's required is that one's essence comes in contact with it, and this magic eats them from the inside out."

I cringed at myself, realizing just how much like my mother I sounded. There could be no question left as to the seriousness of the forces I was about to employ, though. If Ainsley was going to help, and if I was going to trust him to help, he needed to be completely informed as to what he was signing up for.

"Sounds like something that would come in handy right now," he said without flinching.

"Such a dark power should be used sparingly, don't you agree? If word got out that such a thing even existed..."

"If you want me to keep my mouth shut, just say it."

"Fine. Ainsley, if I tell you the plan, can you keep your mouth shut?"

He leaned in, the sudden grave look on his face wiping out any concern I might have had about his ability to take this seriously. "Yes, Queen Fawna. I recognize that we need to dip into some seriously dark shit to win this fight. I also realize how tempting that kind of magic is to some of the garbage swimming around down here. Whatever you tell me doesn't leave this room. I just want to stop Mami Watta."

"Once again, Ainsley, it seems we're in agreement."

I got up from my seat and swam around to the back side of the throne. "This stays a secret as well," I informed him as I tilted the heavy seat, revealing the hidden chamber beneath it.

"Of course the evil queen had her very own secret dungeon," he scoffed. "Your mother I mean. You don't seem so bad."

I couldn't help but smile at the latter part of his statement as I descended into the dark room, which seemed untouched from the last time I had the pleasure of being there. The same cauldron still bubbled with a golden liquid, providing just enough light to see anything at all. Stacks of books and pieces of parchment glowed from their magical protective barrier. Thrown haphazardly around the room, they caught my interest a little more this time, probably because I now had the authority to peruse each and every page if I so desired. Maps pinpointing the strange new places I'd only recently discovered, along with a few I'd yet heard of, clung to the rock wall like wallpaper.

The mess made my stomach sink. There were hundreds of books and I'd have to flip through each and every one of them to find the one hiding the dagger. The exhausting thought made me groan aloud, and just as the sound left my lips a spark of bright blue electricity zapped through the water, stinging my forearm as it whizzed by just close enough to make sure it caught my attention.

"Look out!" Ainsley's grip closed on my upper arm as he yanked me down to the sea floor.

Gritty sand worked its way into my palms. I ignored the biting sting, intent to keep my focus on the single strange blue lightning bolt shooting all over the room. The hair on my arms stood up, aroused by a sudden rush of déjà vu. A hard wave swelled in the dungeon-like room, sloshing the water around us until it caught the bizarre anomaly and directed its flightpath.

Mother. I felt her memorable presence; it clouded the room like a dense fog, filling my lungs with every flap of the gills.

The light smashed into what seemed at first to be a random book, imploding on impact into fireworks that were quickly swallowed up by the choppy water. I forced myself to swim to the spot, and as I got closer I realized the book had the same worn-out cover as the one from my vision.

"This is it," I called over my shoulder to the finman.

He was quick to my side, his eyebrows drawn together as he took in the ordinary-looking object. "I don't mean to burst your bubble, Fawna, but I think that's just a book. Doesn't even look like a spell book."

"Looks that way, doesn't it?" I quirked up the corner of my mouth into a sly smile as I slid my index finger along the creases of the pages. My fingernail found the spot where the spacing felt off, and I peeled back half the pages until the knife revealed itself.

I took the shabby handle in my hand and held up the dirtied blade for inspection. The thick, sticky layer of black potion bubbled on the metal, practically sizzling with potency. A buzzing warmth spread through my hand and up my arm as the enchanted weapon felt me out.

Ainsley stepped forward, glazed over eyes fixed on the artifact in my hand. He approached in a trance, reaching out to run his fingertip down the sharp end of the knife. I jerked it back, and he jumped.

"What are you doing?" I asked, shocked. "One touch, Ainsley. That's all it takes, remember?"

"I don't..." He looked at me, then the knife, then rubbed the back of his neck with the same hand that almost ended his life. "I can't explain it. It's like it was talking to me, telling me to touch it."

"Give me your knife's sheath."

"What? What's wrong with yours?"

I pointed to my empty torso. "As much time as you've spent in my kingdom and with Jewel you haven't noticed that unlike finfolk, we don't carry knives with us everywhere we go?"

"Okay, but I do carry one everywhere and I need the sheath for mine."

"Your knife isn't going to hypnotize someone into committing suicide. We need to keep this out of sight until we need it." I held out my empty hand.

"Fine," he grumbled, unbuckling the belt around his waist that held his personal blade in place. Once he'd removed his own weapon, he tossed the empty holster into my expecting hand.

"Thank—"

Before I could utter my gratitude the entire castle started to quake. A thunderous boom exploded somewhere on the upper level. I flinched from the sound, and Ainsley instinctively placed himself between me and the doorway. The gesture made me gawk at him, and the similarities between his warrior stance and the one Lennox wore in Mami's dungeon were remarkable. Fin-men truly were bred from birth to fight and defend.

"You should stay here," he suggested with just enough finality in his voice to tell me it was more of an order.

I pushed past him, swimming back in the direction of the throne room. "Like hell I will. This is my kingdom, and I'm not going to hide like a rat while we're under attack!"

He hollered something, but I was already too far ahead to make out his protest.

Kicking my tail, I propelled myself forward with enough force to peel through the water. Through the throne room and toward the entryway, I sailed through the water so quick my stomach lurched. I stopped just short of exiting the castle, struck by the silence outside. No screams, no further explosions. Just dead quiet.

The door to the castle had been blown off in Mami's previous attack; any sounds would easily make their way into the castle. If the sea witch came for us again, she'd managed to take them all out with one single blast. I lingered in the doorway, afraid to look outside.

Ainsley finally caught up, his human-like legs

kept him from keeping pace with me. He glared at me, his reddened face showing his embarrassment at that fact. "Thanks for waiting for me," he huffed, out of breath. "What're you waiting for? Go since you're in such a big rush!"

"Shut up, Ainsley, and listen."

He did for a moment, then shrugged. "I don't hear anything. That can't be good."

"Do you think she let loose another mist? Maybe they're all asleep out there."

"There wasn't an explosion when the mist came in Finfolkaheem. We're not going to figure it out loitering in the doorway all day. Want me to go first?"

He moved to step outside, but I pressed a hand against his chest. "No, I should... I should see."

Ainsley snorted then swept his open palm in the direction of the exit. "After you then, Your Majesty."

CHAPTER 19

The sound of distant chatter caught me as soon as I swam outside. The streets were empty, but I followed the noise to Mother's old cargo ship, now reduced to a pile of discarded metal and wood. The closer we came, the louder the voices grew until I let myself hope for the best.

If they were talking, that meant they were alive.

Ainsley and I rounded a corner, finding the entire clan gathered in one giant circle, surrounding something.

"What is it?" Ms. Star asked.

"I've never seen a creature like it before," another mermaid answered. "Look! It has something under its robe."

The Powers teacher cupped her palms over her lips to shout to the merfolk in the front of the pack, "Don't touch it! You don't know where it came from."

Her confirmation that whatever had their attention was indeed alien was enough to send the others into a frantic frenzy. They shouted over one another, trying to decide if they should kill it or try to communicate.

"Nobody is killing anything," I announced. "Not until I've had a chance to determine what it is."

"Fawna!" Margaret's voice rose above the others. From the center of the cluster of mermaids, she swam up over their heads, waving her arms back and forth. "Hurry! It's Gilcrest."

I gasped and swam over top of the crowd until I saw the familiar gigantic, yellow ears pointing at me below. Swooping down, I threw myself on top of him before my frightened clan could decide to take matters into their own hands.

I ordered, "Stop! This isn't just a creature; he's a friend of mine."

"What is he?" Eileen asked, scrunching up her nose at the cross-breed's grotesque appearance.

"A little of this, a little of that," Ainsley snickered before taking Gilcrest's hand in a firm handshake. "It's good to see you're well, old friend. And I see you've brought company."

Gilcrest pulled his flowing robe aside. Another two-legged being crouched beside him, still covering his head as if braced for an attack. Saturated sandy blond hair bobbed with the natural movement of the ocean, and when it whisked to the side and I caught sight of his face, my heart couldn't decide if it wanted to beat faster or stop entirely.

"I thought it best to keep him hidden until you were present, Queen Fawna," Gilcrest said quietly. "The last time these mermaids saw humans walk among us, your mother ruled here. There would be no way to know how they might react to seeing one again."

Without a word, I bent on my tail, dropping to the sea floor in front of Randy. My entire body shook as I reached out to run my fingertips along his scruffy cheek. He flinched, jerking to look at his assailant head on. When his eyes met mine, I couldn't stop the burst of elation from bringing me to tears. Collapsing, I fell into his chest, weeping into his bare skin without a shred of restraint.

Randy's arms folded around me, pulling me so tight against his chest my body cramped from the pressure. The pain just made his presence seem all the more real. He took me by the shoulders and pushed me back to run his eyes along the length of me before he kissed me. My lips quivered against his, finding the perfect spot in the crease of his mouth where we fit together.

"But... but, how are you here?" I managed between sobs that shook my entire body. "Mami Watta has the others. Why didn't she take you?"

He gathered a handful of my hair in his fist and dragged me against him again. I nestled into him, afraid if I loosened my grip even a little he might disappear.

"I tried to save them, Fawna," he told me. His eyes flickered toward the audience still surrounding us. Lost in my unexpected reunion, I had forgotten they were there at all.

Reluctantly, I released Randy's torso only to grab his hand before we could lose contact. "Come on. Gilcrest, you too. We obviously have quite a bit to talk about."

Regis ushered us a path through the crowd of spectators, and I led them to the castle. Once inside the throne room, I waved at Ainsley to close the door. Margaret watched me sit on the throne, her eyes piercing as though she expected me to sprout my mother's disposition the second my backside hit the gold.

It was Randy who spoke up about the odd sight. "Whoa, Fawna. Is this what I think it is? Are you queen now?"

"As I said, Randy, we have a lot to talk about. First, I need to know how you got away."

"With Gilcrest's help," he nodded toward the motionless fin-man-merrow. "I saw the mist coming. I tried to warn your sisters, but they were too far away. I'm sorry, Fawna, I tried to save them. They were on the lower level of Angelique's palace and I was so high up. My legs... I couldn't swim fast enough."

"It's okay," Margaret assured him before I could. "You don't exactly have fins."

I nodded. "She's right. None of this is your fault, Randy."

He swallowed hard, looking to Gilcrest to continue the story.

"Your friend sought me out," Gilcrest explained. "He rushed to warn me of the danger approaching, but as I'm sure you've guessed, I saw it coming."

"If you saw it coming then why didn't you warn the others," Regis demanded.

"It isn't my place to intervene in what fate reveals to me. I have a gift to see but not the ability to act. We all have our curses. This is mine."

Ainsley tapped his chin with his index finger, looking perplexed. "Then why'd you save the human?"

"Hey," I darted up, ready to defend Randy and his rescuer. "You have no right to interrogate Gilcrest for his heroic act."

"I rescued the human," Gilcrest went on in spite of me, "because he was never supposed to be a part of this. Through no fault of his own, he's outside his world, outside his understanding. He has no part in this war. Young Randy is a casualty I could not allow. We sought refuge in the most remote part of the ocean until I felt you return here."

"You should've seen it, Fawna," Randy marveled. "Gilcrest created this vortex thing, like a tunnel that transports you from one place to another. Like a really fast underwater escalator! One minute we were in Finfolkaheem waiting to get swallowed up by that fog and the next, whoosh! We were... well, I don't really know where but someplace safe."

I laughed, his excitement lightening my heart more than words could say. His fascination with my world tickled me down to the core. "I've seen the tunnels the fin-men can create. They're marvelous to say the least."

"Wait a second," Regis interrupted. "This thing is a fin-man?"

"Regis!" Margaret swatted her brother, glaring at him.

"He looks nothing like any fin-man I've ever seen."

"Mind yourself. You're being rude."

Gilcrest released a tired breath, and my heart pitied the look of absolute boredom on his plain face. To grow so used to being insulted it no longer elicited any reaction at all must be a terrible thing.

"Your concern is unnecessary," he stated, whether to Margaret or myself I couldn't tell. "I'm a cross between a fin-man and a merrow. The one and only being of my kind in existence, and if the ocean is a kind caretaker there will never be any more created."

"Don't say such a thing," I scolded. "Your talents are useful beyond compare. To me, you've proven to be simply invaluable."

"Is that what the boom was?" Ainsley wondered. "Your tunnel closing?"

Gilcrest offered a single, disinterested nod.

"I've never heard anything like that, and I've been making those tunnels all my life."

"Consider it a testament to his power," I said.

Margaret opened her mouth to speak, but something on my person caught her attention. She tilted her head, entranced, and swam over to me. Her deft fingers found Ainsley's belt around my waist. From it, the polluted knife dangled in its holster.

The merrow nibbled on her chapping lips, eyeing the weapon with a look of absolute reverence and fear. "You found it."

"That's right."

"You know what that's going to do to you!"

A rush of bubbles followed Randy as he stomped over to me, wrapping a protective arm around my shoulders. "What's going on?"

"It's the only way to defeat Mami Watta, Margaret."

"You can't sacrifice your soul to—"

"We've been over this! I'll sacrifice whatever I

have to if it means getting my child and my sisters back."

"This is how it starts," Regis said. "Nothing evil ever starts out that way."

Randy stepped in front of me, shielding me from their well-intended blows. "Whoa, whoa. Let's get one thing straight. Fawna doesn't have a single bone in her body capable of evil."

"Let's hope you're right, human," Gilcrest chimed in. "Because the hour of reckoning is closer than any of us thought."

I pressed my palms against Randy's shoulders, raising myself above him to see the seer. "What are you talking about, Gilcrest? You said we had until the full moon. That's four days away still."

"Your little detour into the witch's territory set her on high alert. Her original plan was to harness the energy of the full moon, call on it to complete the ceremony. Now, desperation has overcome her senses. She thinks she can harvest the magic inside two royal mermaids with the same result."

"What?" Margaret's shriek barely registered. My scalp prickled as dread sank its teeth into my veins, sealing my gills shut and stealing the oxygen from my lungs. "That... couldn't work. Could it?"

"Of course not. The energy within a being, even two mermaids from a particularly magical bloodline, doesn't even begin to compare to the power nature holds."

"Then she's wasting their lives for nothing," Margaret cried.

I held up a finger, waggling it around like some

brilliant idea could save us all. "She can't leave the water. Neither can her minions. Unless the moon is full, she can't pull this off."

"She doesn't need to be entirely on land to complete the ceremony," Gilcrest explained. "She needs to have a hold of dry earth."

"The shoreline," Ainsley shouted. "She can do it right where the waves crest. One hand on the earth, but close enough to the water to dive back in when she needs to breathe."

"She'll be expecting an attack," Regis claimed.

"No, she doesn't know Gilcrest is helping us," Margaret countered. "She probably thinks Fawna will spend the next few days hiding out, training with me."

I rubbed my temples and paced the throne room. Quieting my mind was the only way to ensure I didn't do anything reckless. It was simple. I'd stick to my original plan. The quicker this was done and over with the better, as far as I was concerned. Besides, this could work in my benefit. Without the energy of the full moon, there was no way she could keep tabs on her ghostly minions while she performed the ceremony and concentrated on breathing.

"When is she planning to do this?" I implored Gilcrest.

"Tomorrow night."

I whirled around, facing Regis and Margaret. "Then we have no time to discuss alternatives. Each of you, find a room for the night. Margaret, any chance you could put together some of that delicious calamari? If this is by chance my last meal, I'd like to enjoy it."

She smiled before a guilty look flashed across her face. "Except for Mami Watta and her dinner, this isn't going to be anybody's last meal. Have a cauldron I could borrow?"

"Definitely. Let's make this a feast. Tomorrow, I take a tunnel to Morocco."

CHAPTER
20

"I 've arranged for Elaine to swim you until you're close enough to shore," I told Randy. I swam in front of a mirror, brushing my white hair until it smoothed so fine it shined. That was one thing I could thank my late mother for. She definitely gave me good hair. Every one of my sisters inherited the healthy keratin, even if we all had different colors.

Margaret didn't let any of us down on the food front. She cooked and fried for the entire clan until every citizen rubbed their full bellies with contentment. If this were to be my last night in this glorious ocean, it was a good one. The only thing that could've made it better would be if the rest of our family was here.

Randy rested on the jutted bedrock in my new quarters, shifting uncomfortably on its hard surface. "God I miss pillows. Sorry, what now? Close enough for what?"

"For you to swim to land once your gills disappear. You're a strong swimmer, so I'm sure you'll do fine. Your boat... I'm sorry you lost it coming after me. Gilcrest was right; you weren't meant to get involved in any of this. Margaret helped me find the

185

spell book containing the potion that would let you go home. We made a batch."

He sat up quick, his forehead wrinkled from his squinting. "I'm not leaving you, Fawna."

The distance between us was small, so it only took a flick of my tail to get to him. I settled on his lap, lacing my fingers at the back of his neck. "Look at me, Randy. You can't stay here."

"No. You don't understand. I thought I'd lost you, Fawna. When the mist came to Finfolkaheem, I thought for sure if she was strong enough to send something like that then that sea witch took you out. Gilcrest wouldn't tell me anything! I just found you again. If you think I'm letting you out of my sight again you're out of your mind."

I leaned my forehead against him, sighing. "You're not suited for this battle, not down here. If you stay I could lose you forever."

"You can't ask me to run away from this. If I go back I would spend the rest of my life wondering if you survived. You're asking me to abandon Sebastian. I love him, too, you know? If anything happens to him..."

"Nothing is going to happen to Sebastian. I won't let it. When this is over I'll find you and tell you the entire story from start to finish. There's no reason for you to risk your life, too."

"You aren't going to come back on land. I see it in your eyes, Fawna. You're not coming home. You are home."

"You're right. I can't leave my people." I blinked back tears. After everything we'd been through, I couldn't lie to him.

"And I can't leave you."

I took a stray piece of his sandy blond hair and twirled it between my fingers. "I don't deserve this kind of loyalty, Randy. You have no idea what I really am."

"I've spent the last year falling more and more in love with you every day."

His lips brushed my jawbone, then slowly down to my jugular. I tilted my head up, lengthening my neckline to savor the warmth of his breath. Randy's soft, tickling kiss teased every nerve in my body until the skin tingled. The ocean couldn't wash away the sensation, not today, not ever.

He pointed to my chest, just over my hammering heart. "I know what's in here, and despite what you've convinced yourself of, you're not a monster, Fawna."

If I held onto his words long enough, could I wish them into being?

No, my deeds had already been done. And if I expected him to let go of what we were—what he thought I was—Randy was going to have to learn the truth. The whole of it.

I summoned up as much strength as I could muster, bringing my arms between us to push him away. "I have to show you something."

Without question, he took my hand, and I led him through the castle and into the throne room. Curiosity lit up his face as he watched me tilt back the throne. To him, I'm sure the scene was something out of a storybook; hidden passageways leading to untold secrets known only to those who knew where to look. There would be no way for him to know what horrors awaited him.

The cauldron boiled steady, the light it emitted more than enough for him to see the oddities strewn about. Just like Ainsley, he marveled at the antiques. Tapping on the hardcover of one of the spell books, he knelt down to inspect the artificial glow it cast off.

"It's magic," I explained. "The only way to preserve the parchment down here. The water would eat it away otherwise."

"Incredible," he exclaimed, mouth agape.

"The maps are lined in it, as well."

Eventually his attention turned to the cauldron. "Is that a potion?"

"Yes, but I don't know what it's for. It's been bubbling that way since my mother was imprisoned. My Aunt Myrtle used her own. She said this one was tainted, wouldn't go near it."

"It's yours now, isn't it? Now that you're queen."

My chest constricted as he said the title, the same way it did when Elaine used it. This was going to take some getting used to. I traced the rim with my finger, foolishly feeling a strange connection with Mother when I did.

"I suppose it is. Maybe I'll see if Margaret can cleanse it. It'd be nice to give it a second chance."

"Good idea. Keep it in the family."

"Randy..." I paused, taking in the look of admiration on his face. This would be the last time I'd ever see it.

As though he could read my thoughts, my sweet

Randy closed the distance between us to clutch my hands in his own. "Whatever it is, Fawna, you can tell me. Nothing could change the way I feel about you."

I took a deep breath. "Do you... do you remember when I told you that we imprisoned my mother?"

"Sure. You said she'd done something awful then you dashed off."

"That's because she's not the only one guilty of doing terrible things. Especially not in this family."

"Tell me what happened."

"For hundreds of years my clan survived without mermen. We did by kidnapping human sailors and bringing them down here the same way I changed you."

"With a kiss."

"Right. Once he impregnated a mermaid he was... no longer needed. Calypso, my mother, believed males of any species to be inherently evil, so she forbade their existence beyond their usefulness."

Randy's face paled a shade, and he shuffled a step back. "You're saying they were murdered once you had what you needed."

"That's exactly what I'm saying. We existed this way under order. Eddie was the last victim to be brought down here against his will."

"That's how he knew all about your family. It wasn't really because Pauline trusted him more than you trusted me; it was because he saw it all first hand." A short lived relief made him straighten, until another shocking fact took its place. "Your clan was going to kill Eddie?"

"Well, Eddie's story is really more involved than that. Pauline didn't mean to draw him down here, and once she did she kept him a secret from everyone until she found a way to turn him back."

"Except for you, right? As close as you two are, I couldn't imagine her keeping anything from you."

"Our relationship wasn't always this strong. I was a part of a secret resistance, one that Pauline knew nothing about. We operated under Calypso's command in the open so as not to draw suspicion. Pauline wasn't prepared to wait until the moment was right to oppose our mother; she wouldn't put Eddie's life in jeopardy for the sake of secrecy even if she knew about our plans. She was much stronger than any of us. Once Calypso was overthrown, we came to live on land so she could be with Eddie."

"And Angelique, when I caught her in my net. Was she trying to like, hypnotize us or something so we would follow her into the water?"

"No, you met Angelique after the practice stopped. Besides, the process required a special connection between the mermaid and the human, a sort of cosmic bond. In other words, I couldn't just go pick a random sailor and sing him into a trance. There would have to be something between us that the ocean saw as worthy to allow the deed to be done."

He rubbed the back of his neck, mulling something over in his head. "Did you have Sebastian before or after you came on land?"

"After." I answered quickly, deciding it better to spit it out. He was piecing it together.

"Sebastian's father," he closed his eyes as if doing so could hide him from the truth he'd uncovered, "was a sailor. A human sailor who you... let your mother kill."

"His name was Gene. And I didn't just allow my mother to kill him, Randy. I dragged him up to the surface myself to suffocate him. *Before* Sebastian was born."

"And he was, for lack of a better term, your soul mate?"

"I think that's a good way to describe it, yes."

"So, what does that make me?"

His question caught me off-guard. This man just learned that the girl he'd been seeing for the last year was a murderer, and his first concern was with whether or not I was fated to be with another. I was prepared for the look of fear or even pure hatred, but not the fallen look of betrayal on his face in this moment.

"I... I hoped you were my second chance," I admitted. My breath hitched in my throat. "But, if there's one thing Mami Watta has proven to me, it's that I don't deserve a second chance."

Gathering himself for a moment, Randy shifted his gaze to the sea floor. He kicked at the sand, concentrating on each tiny crushed diamond as if he'd find one that held all the answers.

"So, you understand now, don't you?" I prodded.

He snapped his neck around, glaring at me again, and I wished with everything I had that he would return his icy stare to the sea floor. "What do I understand, Fawna? Please tell me, because I'm not sure I understand any of this."

"Why you have to leave. You don't belong here, with someone like me. You should swim away while you still can."

"Let me ask you something. If you hadn't killed Gene, if you and your little resistance decided to show face before he died, do you think you'd still be together? One big, happy family with Sebastian."

"I can't say. Gene was never very happy down here. He missed his home, I think, and I believe he eventually would've returned there. I might've followed him, but without Pauline I couldn't imagine staying on land for long, and without Eddie, she would have no reason to want to be up there."

My answer seemed to soothe his ache, and he inched a little closer. "And if you'd acted before you did, defied your mother and refused her order to kill him, do you believe you could've won?"

"Honestly? I don't know. It doesn't matter. For all we know, we could've stopped it long before Gene. Aunt Margaret just kept telling us to be patient, that the catalyst would show itself. We rallied against my mother more because Pauline was in danger, not so much because of Eddie. To me, that was the ultimate incentive to proceed. Seeing her in danger was the reason we stood so strong together."

"Maybe your aunt knew a human wasn't a strong enough reason to fight such an epic war. I mean, you might've rallied behind Gene, but could you say the others in your resistance would? With everything Gilcrest has told you, you've got magic in you, Fawna. You stood a chance against your mother. Your aunt probably knew that."

"You may be right, but it doesn't matter. I've committed some terrible atrocities."

"Because you were scared! You didn't have a choice. I wasn't even here and I can see that." He clanged his knuckles against the cast iron frame of the cauldron. "You said you wanted to give this old heirloom a second chance, an opportunity to be used for good. Why can't you give yourself that chance? Cut yourself a break."

A smile cracked on my lips, and I shook my head in exasperation. "Why is it you always insist on seeing the good in me, even now when there's none to be found?"

"There's plenty of good in you, Fawna. If there wasn't, you wouldn't be so ready to risk your soul to rescue the ones you love the most."

"There's no talking any sense into you, is there?" I wrapped my arms around his torso, using his weight to anchor myself in place.

"Not a chance," he grinned, planting a sweet kiss on my cheek. "I'm not going anywhere. It's like I said before, Queen, my heart is yours and only yours. The sea is in my blood, always has been. Now I know why. I was meant for this life, down here with you and Sebastian. Don't take it away from me because of a past you can't outrun. You're going to have to drag me up to the surface yourself, and then figure out a way to get that potion down my throat. That's the only way I'm leaving."

My heart was caving; I could feel it. As much as I wanted Randy topside where he was safe, his refusal to leave was a victory of sorts. A selfish victory that fed my ego and made me feel like finally I was worth something if a man this wonderful was willing to sacrifice so much to stay by my side. My head told me to continue the argument, to push him away until he left on his own accord. My heart, it sang a different tune, and I wasn't strong enough to deny its dire need for my Randy.

Through my lashes, I peered up at him. "Okay."

"Okay?" he echoed.

"I won't fight you on this anymore."

"I see a 'but' coming."

"But," I giggled. He knew me much too well. "You can't come with me to confront Mami Watta."

"No deal," he stepped back, digging his heels in. "You're not going by yourself."

"I didn't say I was going alone. No offense, Randy, but you smell. All humans do. It's a ripe, alien odor that doesn't belong down here and it'll give us away the second we get anywhere near her."

He lifted his arm, sniffing under it. "I don't smell anything."

"That's because *all humans smell the same.* You know that fishy odor you always complained about when we took Pauline to sushi restaurants? I never once smelled it, because I'm from where the fish dwell."

"Guess that explains why you always smelled like an ocean breeze to me."

"Probably so. Besides, the less individuals involved the better. I'm bringing Ainsley because I need his tunnels. Gilcrest's make me sea sick, weird coming from a mermaid, I know."

Randy's right eyebrow shot up. "You're going to fight with that fin-man?"

"No. The fin-man is going to provide me transport, nothing more. He's going to stay away from the shoreline in hiding. I have to be stealthy, sneak up on her while she's concentrating on the spell. There's no other way I can win this."

"Once again, my little mermaid, you cut yourself short."

CHAPTER
21

Margaret fussed over the satchel she put together for my voyage, unpacking and repacking it over and over again. "I don't think there's enough rations in here. What if you get hungry?"

"Then I'll spear myself a fish," I answered.

Elaine gave me a lopsided smile. "Are you sure you remember how to do that?"

"I haven't been gone that long!" I swatted at her with a playful smile. "Don't underestimate the queen."

She curtsied, the look on her face screaming sarcasm. "Pardon me, Your Majesty."

"Ugh," I grumbled. "Stop that. I hate the title."

"It's what you are," Margaret was quick to remind me. "And it's what your people need right now."

"No, what they require is some peace and quiet."

Elaine sighed, and the humor in her demeanor all but disappeared. "I'm not sure they're going to get much of that until you return."

"Come on, you were just so lively! Don't let my departure ruin your mood."

"We're just worried about you."

Margaret squeezed my forearm with her peeling

green fingers, and my chest constricted. This merrow who owed neither me nor my people anything in the ocean had been so kind, so helpful in our time of need. There was no way I could ever repay her.

"Don't mention it," she insisted, flashing a knowing smile. "I knew when I got involved that Angelique would've done the same for me, and after getting to know you, I have no doubt in my mind you would as well."

"Your telepathic abilities are incredible," I remarked.

She blushed. "Sorry, I don't mean to intrude. Sometimes I can't help it."

"I know, Margaret. I don't mind at all."

"Are you sure we can't come with you?" Elaine asked me.

"No, there's one knife and one sea witch. There's no reason to drag anybody else into this fight. Besides, Elaine, I need you here. The clan knows you, they trust you. Keep them calm until I come back."

"You better come back," she countered. "Otherwise I'm leaving your human to rule in your stead."

Margaret couldn't help but snicker. "Could you imagine? A human ruling the kingdom. Your clan would probably riot."

"He's going to rule," I corrected her. "Randy's made his choice. Despite knowing the entire truth about our history and what I've done, he's chosen to stay. I'd say that kind of bravery and devotion earns him a shiny gold throne right next to mine."

"Agreed." Elaine approved with a sharp nod. "It takes a special kind of love to endure the level of shock that poor man's been through."

"Oh I didn't mean—"

Cutting Margaret off, I said, "I know, I know. It's just, this needs to be clear: when I come back, Randy stays."

"Glad to hear you've come to terms with my decision."

I spun around, smiling from ear to ear as I watched Randy walk toward me. "You came."

"Of course I came. You think I'd let you swim off without saying goodbye?"

"Of course not," I lied. In truth, I thought he wouldn't be able to face the very real possibility that I wouldn't be coming back. "It never crossed my mind."

"I brought your ride with me." He scuttled aside, and Ainsley's smaller figure appeared. "He needed a gulp of air before you left."

Fin-men were perhaps the oddest creatures in the ocean to me. Though they looked like humans who glowed from the inside with a bioluminescence flowing through their veins, they behaved more like whales. Relishing in the sea, they required oxygen from the surface to survive, even though they couldn't live outside the water.

The females of their clan, however, had the luxury of surviving in or out of water. The whole species was so full of contradictions it's no wonder the humans living just above their kingdom had such a fascination with the mythology surrounding them.

The fin-man shuffled forward. "I'm under the threat of death to bring you home safely."

"Don't listen to Randy," I scoffed. "He's harmless."

"A man who's in love is capable of just about anything, believe me."

His statement reminded me that he had just as much to lose in this as I did. He loved Jewel the same way Randy loved me. Facing down the dirtiest demon in the sea was a small price to pay as far as he was concerned if it meant rescuing the woman he loved.

Just one more reason this could not fail.

Ainsley opened the pocket of his holster, which dangled around my waist. "Just making sure you didn't forget our ace in the hole."

"I can't believe you're really going to do this," Margaret complained once again. "There's got to be another way."

I rolled my eyes, but it was Randy who responded in my place. "There isn't. Fawna knows you don't like the plan, Margaret, and I know she wouldn't do it if she thought there was any other way. She knows what she's doing."

"Thank you," I breathed. "Where's Regis? I haven't seen him all morning."

"He... won't be here." The merrow tugged at a strand of her tangled black hair. It was obvious that covering for her brother wasn't something she was used to doing. "It isn't that he doesn't appreciate everything you're putting at stake. We all know what will happen if Mami Watta succeeds. It's just, he doesn't approve."

"I understand. And I appreciate you being here

despite your own disapproval."

"I'll be here when you return, Fawna. I promise."

Tugging on the strap of the holster one last time to make sure the knife was secure, I returned my attention to Ainsley.

"Are we ready?"

"I am if you are," he answered.

"Good. Let's get moving. We don't want to get there too late."

As fast as the fin-men tunnels were, we were traveling across the entire ocean. It would take hours to reach our destination, and once we were there I would need to scope out the terrain to find the best vantage point. A long night was spent going over tactics with Regis. The merrow was, after all, the most highly respected scout in his clan.

According to him, while we had the advantage of surprise, Mami Watta would likely still be prepared for the unexpected. My position couldn't be anywhere close to visible, nor could it be so remote that it inhibited my ability to attack in an instant. Not knowing anything about the shores of Morocco would be my own disadvantage, and I needed to have time before her arrival to familiarize myself with it.

My goodbye kiss with my Randy was quick and without passion. Part of me was afraid if I kissed him as though I'd never see him again, it would cement the possibility even more. He seemed to share the sentiment, because he let me go as if I was just swimming away to fetch a flower from the seaweed fields.

Ainsley rolled his hands, a burst of bubbles exploding in the center of them. The disturbance quickly gave way to a small whirlpool, which expanded exponentially quicker than the one Lennox created. This wasn't a testament to Lennox's ability to create the tunnel, I realized. The situations were much different. Ainsley didn't have the burden of needing to be discreet.

Unlike Gilcrest's tunnel, no sonic boom shook the ocean floor. Instead, a quiet rush of water shot in front of him, creating the very transportation vortex we required. This was the third time I'd witnessed such a thing, and I still found myself hypnotized by the magic of it.

Neither of us looked back as we dove headfirst into the waterspout, ready and eager to put an end once and for all to the tyranny threatening our way of life.

The journey between Atargatis and Morocco took longer than either of us expected. Out of respect, I wouldn't tell Ainsley his tunnel rushed at a much slower speed than Lennox's. I could only imagine a fin-man's ability to manipulate water was a great source of pride for them, and I wouldn't bite the hand that transported me. When we emerged on the other side, sunset was upon us.

"You know what to do." I swiped my sweaty palms along my scaly tail. The pain in my stomach was so intense, I could've doubled over. Now that the moment had come, I feared my nerves would be my undoing.

"Yeah," he grumbled. "Swim up to the surface for a gulp of air, then stay here and wait for you like a coward."

"It's got nothing to do with cowardice, Ainsley. Rage is a powerful ally to someone like Mami. You know her distaste for fin-men, and she's going to be vicious enough when she sees me."

"You're asking me to defy my very nature, you understand that don't you? I'm a warrior. Fighting is my blood."

"Yes, I know what I'm asking of you, Ainsley. But if this works I'm going to need you and your tunnel to get me back to her castle to save the others, and then home again. You're not going to be much use to me if you're dead."

"Fine. But if—"

"No. Under no circumstances are you to intervene, do you understand me? If something should go wrong, your job is to get back to Atargatis and warn the others. At least they'll have a fighting chance if they're prepared."

I turned to swim away, terminating the argument once and for all.

"Fawna," he called after me. "Be careful. A lot of us, including me, need you to survive."

His clumsy, human-like legs sloshed against the water as he ascended up. When I couldn't hear it any longer, I swam the opposite direction, down to the sea floor, toward my fate.

I followed the sandy ground until the incline

leading toward the shoreline came into sight. An odd sound began irritating my ear drum, and I froze at once. A rhythmic and repetitive *boom, boom, bang* replayed over and over.

Drums.

On land and by sea, music was an integral part of any ceremony. Something about it touched the soul, intensifying one's desire and heightening one's senses. Mami Watta was near, and lucky for me, her shared appreciation of the art gave her away before I swam right into her.

Rummaging through the bag at my side, I pulled our Regis's magical binoculars. The powerful scopes sliced through the dark water, which judging by the clear view I had, would be crystal clear by day. A splash about a half mile away nabbed my attention, and that's when I saw her.

Mami Watta.

Alive and in the flesh, and best of all, completely unaware of what was about to happen to her.

In her arms she held a bundled heap, one that thrashed and wiggled. Sebastian. She carried my baby close, in an almost tender embrace, careful to keep him from slipping away. Poseidon forbid she lose the one thing she needed above all else to obtain her goal.

His name bubbled in my throat, threatening to seep out in a scream of anguish. I covered my own mouth to keep it from escaping and bit down on my finger. Thank the sea, the fork of my tail went numb, or I might've launched myself at him without thinking.

A few deep breaths slowed my mind enough to regain myself. I'd come this far, and I could never live with myself if I mucked this up because I couldn't control my behavior. Instead, I kept a careful eye on every move Mami made, making note of the fact that there wasn't a ghostly minion in sight. She headed up the incline, struggling with the extra weight of Sebastian.

Unfortunately for her, I had no such cargo to slow me down. Sebastian gurgled a playful, almost joyous sound and a hunger built in my core like nothing I'd felt before. I had to have him back.

I swam up until just my eyes were above the surface. Any flapping of the gills could catch the attention of the wretched old hag who was already on high alert. Jagged, rocky mountains lined the coastline, interrupted by only a small, secluded beach. The moonlight shined down on the empty space like a spotlight, leading straight into a hidden cave almost invisible from the water.

Perfect.

I dug inside my satchel again, this time pulling out the familiar necklace I'd worn around my neck for the last year. The emblem featured a creature that bore a striking resemblance to Ursula from the little mermaid; half woman, half octopus. I ran my fingers along the image, chuckling to myself at how proper the symbol really was. Part of the sea, yet part of the land.

Exactly what Mami Watta wanted for herself, and it would give me the upper hand needed to destroy her.

CHAPTER 22

Once inside, I realized the cave was more like an alcove. It didn't actually go into the mountain, but provided enough cover to serve my purposes. Cobwebs decorated the walls and bats hung from the ceiling. Two of the absolute worst creatures of the human world, I shivered, every now and then swatting at the phantom tickling of spider legs on my skin.

Through Regis's binoculars the cresting waves came in clear. Just beyond them, right about where the sandbar would be, Mami's head finally emerged from the depths. She sang a tune, then deepened her voice to mimic the sound of a drum; the same sound that had brought her presence to my attention in the first place.

She swam closer, struggling as the waves rolled until she rested just on the edge of the beach. The rolling surf crashed into her, as if the sea was trying to pull her back in. Kicking hard, she managed to maneuver out of the ocean's grip to place Sebastian on the damp, sticky sand.

My toes dug into the earth, seeking leverage to sprint forward at a moment's notice. A sickening smacking sound disrupted the serene noise of the ocean. It came from Sebastian's gills as they flapped open and closed, searching for the water. The knife's handle bruised my palms, I squeezed it so tight. That twisted old sea witch wouldn't even give my baby the comfort of breathing. She could put his necklace on, ease his discomfort. But, she was too wrapped up in her own selfish agenda to consider mercy.

I stayed hidden while she lifted her hands toward the sky, asking the gods of the land to bless her transformation. From inside her colorful sleeve, she produced a vile containing a sparkling silver liquid, its color identical to that of the moon. She uncorked the neck of the bottle and downed the potion in one quick swig.

The snake around her neck slithered down her arm until she gripped his neck between her thumb and index finger. He didn't struggle, apparently so used to his handler he had no reason to protest. She kissed his nose, and the soft glow encasing his length flickered out. That's when she released him, and he undulated his way toward Sebastian.

My baby stilled as the snake glided up his tail, flicking his skin with the length of its forked tongue. The scene fogged over, as pure and absolute panic seized my wits. Whatever potion Mami Watta drank, she transferred it to the snake to inflict Sebastian. As though sensing the threat, he hoisted himself up, his tiny fork sinking deep into the compacted sand. No matter how hard he tried, Sebastian had yet to take his first steps, and his little fin couldn't contend with the cement-like suction of the soaked silt.

What he did accomplish, though, was ridding

himself of the magic infested pest. As her beloved pet tumbled to the ground, Mami shouted something indistinct, the loud crashing of the waves muffling her words. The sea slung an angry upsurge at the creature, dragging him back by force and without his bubble of air the sea witch christened him with.

I let out a breath when I saw the ocean nabbed Sebastian, too. His gills submerged long enough for him to suck in a breath before Mami jerked him back out into dry air.

From my baby's lips, a desperate cry pierced the night. One that gave my legs the permission they needed to hurdle toward my crying baby.

I knew better; the veil of night would've offered me more than enough cover if I had just moved slow, but my maternal need to soothe Sebastian went to my head. By the time Mami Watta looked up, I was on top her, tackling her back into the water.

As she tumbled back, Mami dropped Sebastian. From the corner of my eye I watched the tide wrap him up in a shroud of murky safety, sweeping him out of harm's way. Half a second was all I could spare to give the sea my silent thanks, for the sea witch rained down on me with a blasting assault of flesh searing magic. On instinct, my arm snapped back. Recoiling from the pain, I kicked my legs to swim away from her.

Since she still had her tail, she caught up to me without any effort. I twisted around, ready to face her with my secret weapon. At close range, she continued the barrage of magical fireballs, hurling one after the other as I barely dodged each one. I fumbled with the knife, cursing myself for not having it at the ready when I tackled her in the first place. If I'd used my head, this fight would've been over before it even started.

Fighting against the turbulent violence of the sea, I did my best to lunge at her with my weak human appendages, swiping the blade down and across like it was a sword instead of a dagger. She threw her head back and laughed. Evading my attacks was nothing more than child's play for Mami, especially considering I couldn't even get close enough to make the slightest contact.

"Stupid girl," she taunted. "A simple knife couldn't do so much as make me bleed. I'm immortal, immune to any weapon you could pull out of that silly satchel."

The remaining fireball in her palm burned out, and she swooped her hand in my direction. An invisible force launched me down, off the incline and into deeper water. With nothing more than the sorcery she conjured, she held me under, her black eyes boiling with delight as I bucked and kicked, trying my hardest to get loose. The chain securing my pendant knotted around itself, tight and choking. If I couldn't remove it, I wouldn't last long before I drowned in the very substance that gave me life and a home for all but one of my years. She squeezed tighter, concentrating on my wrist until I dropped the knife. Helplessly, I watched my salvation drift to the seafloor.

My cheeks burned and my lungs begged for air. Just as I was sure I would pass out, Mami hauled me up again, loosening her grip just enough to allow the tiniest bit of air to trickle in. She wanted me to suffer, I saw it written all over her face. The wretched witch would probably waterboard me for hours until my body shut down from the trauma.

"That's right," she responded to my thoughts. "You're going to suffer just as much as your mother did. Would you like to know how I killed her, Fawna dear?"

My legs dangled over the water, my toes scraping the briny safe haven below. I gurgled and squeaked, but the pressure on my throat was too much to squeeze out a single word. Only Mami's torso was visible, with her bottom half underwater and hidden by the dark of night.

"I aired her out, just as she did to those disgusting humans. Only, not all at once. No. I made sure she deteriorated bit by bit, until her agony was so unbearable she begged me to kill her. Could you imagine it? The great Queen Calypso, begging for anything at all. It seems unthinkable, I know, but I assure you she did."

Her words hit me like a punch to the stomach. The amount of pain and anguish it would take to get my mother to beg must've been horrendous. I'd never even heard her so much as ask someone for something. Imagining the scene overwhelmed me, causing a wave of nausea that could've brought me to my knees had I not been paralyzed in Mami's hold.

"But you, my dear. I think we both know you're not going to last as long as she did. Not even close."

My shallow breathing quickened, a blistering

wrath building in my core.

"I've been watching you, you know. Your entire life you've lived in the shadow of both your sisters. Angelique has your mother's strength, pure and sturdy. Your youngest sister, well, she may be meek and quiet, but she's as stubborn as Calypso. And what are you, Fawna? A weak, feeble little mermaid much too afraid to lead anything. Even when you joined that pathetic excuse for a resistance, you hid from the spotlight. With the entire group of opposers behind you, you still let them kill poor Gene, didn't you?"

My fists squirmed free of her grasp, and my fingers trembled as a heat started in my palm. I concentrated on it, using Mami's words to feed the magic I knew was in there deep down. She kept talking, continued the barrage of insults and deprecation, and with every word my hatred fed the flames.

"And your sisters," she added, "I promise you, they'll suffer the same fate as you and your mother. They'll die slowly because you couldn't just swim away. Their blood is on your hands, Fawna. Along with every member of your clan who will suffer because you insisted on resisting fate."

Warmer and warmer, the fireball in my hand ignited, licking away the flesh. I jolted my arm forward, wriggling it free from the sea witch's strong hold, but she was too far into her monologue to take notice.

"And Randy," she continued, "I haven't decided what cruelty should befall his head yet. He will, however, be my favorite victim. Your second chance." She pouted her lips, mocking me. "Merfolk like us don't get second chances."

Concentrating on my thoughts, I tapped into my weak telepathic abilities. She may have stolen my voice, but I'd be damned if she wasn't going to hear what I had to say.

"How wrong you are, Mami Watta."

She cocked her head at me, surprised by the mental intrusion. "What did you say?"

"I said, you're wrong. My mother gave you your second chance when she put you in charge of the ushering of the dead. Instead of using your power to aid the lost and confused, you chose to take the corrupt path once again. You squandered your second chance. I won't waste mine."

The fireball in my hand pulsated, and I winced from the intensity. The sea witch cackled at my optimism, and I took her distraction as opportunity, flinging my own magic at her full speed. Just like in the Kingdom of Merrows, it landed with a volatile impact.

It hit Mami Watta right in the chest, throwing her from the sea entirely. Her limp body crashed into one of the stone foothills with such force an avalanche of rock and boulders crumbled. She landed on the beach with a hard thud, the debris sliding into place to bury her alive.

"Holy Poseidon," I breathed, falling to my knees as I heaved in air. My heart pounded against my ribcage, and my entire body shook from the shock of my own strength.

Old and feeble, the likelihood that she could unbury herself was slim to none, but with the power she held I wasn't about to take any chances. I lapped up another mouthful of oxygen before I dipped my head under water. In my human form, the saltwater burned my eyes, but I forced myself to fight through the discomfort to find that blasted dagger.

An unnatural, miniscule squall twisted on the floor, brushing aside a thin layer of silt. Under it, a dull gleam twinkled. Once again, I offered the ocean my heartfelt appreciation for her help. I'd always learned the sea doesn't choose sides, but this night she seemed to make an exception.

I swam toward it, my legs aching from the use of muscles I'd forgotten how to use. When I had it in my clutches, I returned to the surface, and the rising tides seemed to push me straight to the spot where the landslide held Mami Watta prisoner.

As I leaned over the wreckage, a bolder shot upward, missing my head by mere inches. A wrinkled hand appeared, reaching for me as if I might help the same individual who just threatened to murder me and my entire family. I stared down at her through the newly created cavity that gave me a clear view of her face. My face remained as stone.

Mami moaned, incapable of concealing her battered condition. "Help me, child. Please, I need to get back in the water."

"Or what?" I crouched down, sneering at her. "You're immortal, remember? Nothing can kill you."

"No, it won't be my end that's true. But without the water I'll breathe sandpaper for the rest of my days." She hacked a half-convincing cough.

"Why, Mami Watta, would I even think of helping you? I could swim away right now, release my sister from your prison. I should leave you here to suffer the way my mother suffered by your hand."

"Someone would find me eventually."

I unsheathed the knife, flashing it in front of her face. "Not if you're nothing but ash."

"Again with the primitive weaponry? You're even stupider than I—"

"It's not a simple blade." I pointed to the black blemishes on the edge, slowly running my finger from the tip to the base. "My mother's been saving this just for you, Mami Watta."

In her tiny crevice, the sea witch tried to inch back. Her tail flopped wildly, and a dreadful fear flashed across her face. Then, just as quick as she became agitated, she settled again.

"You've not enough of your mother's blood in you to do such a thing. I've seen your heart, Fawna. You're a pure soul."

"Once upon a time, my soul may have been as innocent as you claim, but you tarnished it the day you took my son from me. I took my own mother down because she tried to separate us, or did your vision miss that part, Mami?"

I detained her flailing arm in an iron grip, grazing her skin with the blade's tip just enough to draw blood, a wound large enough to absorb the poison. This didn't need to be a brutal attack, just effective enough to get the job done. Her dark cheeks faded to an ashen color, and I knew it was enough.

"You see?" She half-smiled. "Here you have me defenseless, and still you can't take your aim."

"You mistake my restraint for mercy. Unlike you and my mother, I take no joy in taking a life. Even one as terrible as yours."

She gasped and grabbed at her heart. The potion was mixing with her blood now. The tendons in her neck swelled as she fought for air, and her hands moved to her neck. "What... what have you done?"

"What I must do to keep the ocean safe from creatures like you."

Her skin split as the poison ate her away from the inside out. She screamed a cry of pure agony, and as much as I hated her, I knew the sound would haunt me for the rest my days. Molecule by molecule, I watched her disintegrate until nothing remained of the great and powerful Mami Watta but dust beneath a pile of rubble.

CHAPTER
23

The waves lapped at my ankles, calmer now, as if the sea knew the fight was over. I swiped away a single tear of guilt, the one and only I would allow myself to shed. Holding out my hand, I turned it in the moonlight, inspecting my skin for a sign of newfound darkness.

I didn't feel evil.

Maybe Poseidon would grant me forgiveness, just this once.

Fiddling with the necklace around my neck, I waded out into the water and closed my eyes. The foam frothed around my knees, and I thought of the last time I did this—just outside my apartment. The ocean cried for my attention then, and now that I'd answered her plea, she welcomed me home.

I pulled off the pendant and tucked it safely into my satchel. As my toes webbed themselves together, transforming into fins, I took comfort in knowing this was the last time I'd feel the sensation. My time on land was over, but my reign under the waves was just beginning.

Smiling wide, I dove under, casting my telepathic voice far and wide. Sebastian was no longer in danger, but I had no idea where the waters took him to keep him safe. The tiniest giggle answered me back, and I swam toward it as fast as my tail would carry me.

"Hey, hold still," Ainsley called out. "Your mother's going to be back soon, all right? Just stay in one spot, would you?"

Peace and playfulness battled for my heart's attention as I watched the fin-man scuffling his feet to try and keep up with my little merman. His time with the sea witch didn't slow him down any. Sebastian zipped about, swimming circles around his pursuer.

"Are you giving my friend a hard time?" My baby stopped the second he heard my voice and something fluttered in my chest.

"Mommy!" He swam for me, slamming into my chest with his arms open wide.

I held him close, shimmering tears of joy streaming down my face as I kissed the top of his head and swaddled him side to side. He pointed to my fin, and I could only imagine what kind of questions danced around in his young mind. This world was all so new to him, but soon enough his roots would bring him the same sort of comfort it brought me.

"I tried to keep an eye on the little guy," Ainsley said with a sheepish grin. "He's fast."

"Yes, he is," I cooed in a high-pitched mommy voice, more at Sebastian than Ainsley. "He's so fast and so brave, aren't you, Sebastian?"

The merling nodded his little blonde head.

"So, it's done?"

"It is," I confirmed. "Mami won't be bothering us

anymore."

He patted my back in the manliest fashion possible. "Good job. Should we drop him off in Atargatis before we go spring the others out of her dungeon?"

"Are you kidding me? I'm not letting this little boy out of my sight ever again."

"That's sure going to be a bummer when he's trying to pick up mermaids. Poor guy."

"He's got some time to adjust to the idea," I teased. "Come on, Sebastian. Let's go break your aunties out of jail, huh?"

"This place is a ghost town," Ainsley complained as we wandered through the corridors of Mami's dungeon.

"I think you mean a town without ghosts," I countered.

It was indeed a strange sight, especially since the last time we were here the castle was teeming with undead. Not a single ghostly minion loitered in Mami's kingdom now, inside or out. Mother, and all the others, were gone. Now, without a merrow to light the way with one of their orbs, I did my best to keep a fireball lit to help. Sebastian's fingers curled around the fin of my tail, and I dragged him along as we went.

Ainsley tapped on the cement wall, checking for voids beneath its surface. "Where do you think they all disappeared to?"

"I guess when I killed Mami it broke her bond

with them. Which I suppose means they're wherever they're supposed to go beyond here."

"That's helpful."

"I'll tell you what, since you're the warrior between us, you'll probably end up dying first. You come back and let me know where that is."

"I'm the warrior? You're the one who took out the sea witch, remember?"

"Killing isn't a habit I'm looking to get into. You can keep that hobby."

"I have a feeling Jewel is going to feel the same way. After all this, she's probably going to be scared of her own shadow."

I guffawed, shaking my head. "You don't know Jewel all that well, do you? That mermaid doesn't know the meaning of fear. She crawled up on land, naked and with no idea where she was going, just to tell Pauline and me about what happened in Atargatis. She's not a coward; don't insult her like that."

"You're right," Ainsley admitted. "It's just a stereotype we have about mermaids, that's all. Sort of how you all think fin-men are mindless, bloodthirsty killing machines."

"Touché, fin-man."

We exchanged knowing smiles, a silent apology for our ignorance of one another. So help me, the rift between our clans would be mended under my rule. Angelique and I would behave as allies, set an example for our citizens to follow.

The dragging weight behind me lightened, and I whipped my head back to search for Sebastian. He zoomed under me, swimming ahead with a mischievous grin.

I took chase, yelling, "Sebastian, come back here!"

"Told you he was fast."

He was, and it took all the energy I had left in my exhausted body to swim fast enough to keep him in my line of sight. Sebastian rounded a corner, and goosepimples peppered my arms. The thought of losing him again consumed me, and adrenaline coursed through my veins.

Not again, I told myself as my fear reignited my oomph.

I twisted around the corner, colliding into iron cell bars. My body vibrated from the sudden stop and my shoulder throbbed from the impact.

"Still know how to make an entrance, don't you, big sister?" Angelique pressed her face between the slats, smirking at me. "No offense, but I think your merling is more graceful than you are."

Pauline sat on bended tail at her side, holding Sebastian's chubby little hand with hers. Jewel and Lennox stood behind them, their eyes wide with surprise. Gawking at them, my mouth hung open and my mind raced to find words.

"You're here!" Jewel jumped in, half-laughing and half-sobbing.

Ainsley's rushed footsteps came into the room, screeching to a halt when he entered. "Of course we're here," he announced. "You think I'd just let you rot in here, beautiful? Not a chance."

"But how?" Pauline implored.

Lennox came up to the cell door, placing his

hand against the small of Angelique's back. "Your sister took out the big bad witch, that's how."

"Is it true?" Angelique asked.

A lump in my throat strangled me, but I managed to answer, "Yes. It's true. She's gone."

"I knew you would," Pauline insisted, her purple eyes twinkling. "But still, I was so worried."

"Mother... Mother is gone, too. I couldn't get to her in time."

"Mother was gone before we even got here," Angelique informed me. "I saw her spirit out there as Mami brought us in."

"I'm sorry," I said softly. "I know the two of you were growing closer. This will hurt you the most, I think."

"It was a long time coming, Fawna. It's nothing you did or didn't do. Mother had enemies all over the world. Eventually one was going to nab her."

"She's right," Pauline agreed. "This isn't your fault. None of it is. You saved us, Fawna. All of us, plus those poor ghosts that sea witch held prisoner. You did good."

"Exactly. Now, would you mind doing one more good deed and get us out of this cage?"

CHAPTER
24

I leaned as close as I could to the mirror, trying to see past the rusted cracks and tragic scratches marring the surface of it. Aside from the heavy dark circles under my eyes, I didn't look any different. On the inside, as hard as I searched, I couldn't find the darkness in my soul that should be festering there.

But, maybe that was the thing. Maybe you didn't feel the evil creep into your heart because it snuck in, twisting its way into your being until it was too late. Maybe you were supposed to be unaware of its presence.

The modest tiara resting on my head sparkled. Mother would hate it, I decided. She'd say it was too small, too plain for someone of our royal blood. But for me, it was perfect. It was there to remind me who was in charge, but not so flashy I would lose sight of myself. I would hold on to the little thing and what it represented to me. Maybe it would keep me from stumbling unto Mother's path.

Pauline's purple hair bounced in the background, catching my attention.

"You're going to stare a hole in your forehead," she teased. "Stop looking for something that isn't there. You're still the same impossibly moral and devoted sister."

"Please. I don't think anyone could mistake me for moral. But, thank you."

"You know, I can't believe you aren't going to wear Mother's crown. It was bequeathed to you, you know. It's been in our family for generations."

"It's much too bulky for my taste. It'll look much nicer on display in the throne room where everyone in Atargatis can view it and remember where we came from."

"Are you sure it doesn't have anything to do with the fact that wearing it would make you immortal?"

"Immortality is a dangerous gift, Pauline. One that frankly, I don't believe anyone is entitled to. I'd destroy that relic if I could, but since I can't, I'll just have to settle for the spell Margaret put on it for me."

She quirked a brow at me. "What spell?"

"One that curses any creature who dares place it upon his or her head. They'll turn into a snake if they do. I thought it fitting."

"That sounds like something you ought to tell your sisters!"

"If neither of them intend on trying to steal the throne from under my nose then what should it matter?" I pointed out with a smirk.

"You've already gone mad with power," Pauline joked. "I knew it was only a matter of time."

I laughed then swam by her, taking her hand in mine as I left the room. "Come on. We better catch your ride before Lennox and Angelique leave."

The thought of ruling Atargatis was frightening

enough, but knowing that I would have to do it with one sister on land and the other about as far north as one could get was almost heart-stopping. Angelique had her own responsibilities as queen of her own kingdom, and deep down I knew what Eddie and Pauline had was a once in a life time kind of love. She couldn't breathe without him much longer, and I would never stand in the way of her happiness.

Truth be told, I had no idea if I was fit for the job or not, but as I swished toward my Randy, who held Sebastian on his hip and pointed toward a colorful school of fish, I knew I'd be okay. He insisted on staying with me, claiming everyone on land already probably thought he was lost at sea anyway. If I had my boys, I could face down whatever the ocean threw my way.

Angelique and Lennox waited in the courtyard. Their eagerness to return home radiated off them. As we approached, Lennox tapped his foot on the ocean floor. When my sister saw me, her eyes lit up and she smiled wide in a proud way she never had before. I'd capture that smile in my memory forever.

"You'll make sure Pauline arrives safely, won't you?" I handed my youngest sister over to my middle sister, my skin already cold from the loss. I would see them both again, that much was certain, but it just wouldn't be the same.

"Of course," Angelique confirmed with a patient grin. "We'll drop her off on our way back to Finfolkaheem. I'll keep an eye on her until I see her walking on those two hideous legs."

"Good. Pauline, did you remember to pack your

amulet? You'll need it or you won't—"

Pauline brushed a strand of my white hair out of my eyes, shushing me. "This isn't my first landfall, Fawna. I'll be fine. I have everything I need."

"Right, sorry."

Randy walked up next to me, draping his arm around my shoulders and placing a soft, understanding kiss on my temple. I clung to him, rubbing noses with my baby who looked at this human with such admiration in his eyes, it was inconceivable that they weren't father and son.

"You're going down in history, you know." Lennox nodded in my direction. "The finfolk have been trying to figure out a way to take down Mami Watta our entire existence. My people are already hailing you for your victory."

I shook my head and said, "I don't want my legacy to be one of murder, Lennox. Tell your people if they must remember me, to remember me as an ally of the ocean. Nothing more."

"I'll relay the message."

The fin-man flicked his wrist, creating the powerful vortex that brought our worlds together. This time when he left, Ainsley would stay behind. Partly an ambassador of his clan, but mostly a protector of his beloved Jewel. He wouldn't let her out of his sight even now that the danger was gone.

We said our tearful good-byes, and I watched them disappear into the dizzying whirlpool, leaving our kingdom in my trusted hands. I could only hope I would live up to their expectations, that my legacy would be as memorable as my mother's.

This time, though, I wouldn't let hate or fear win.

"What now, my queen?" Randy asked me in a sweet, enthusiastic voice.

I plucked Sebastian from his arms, bouncing him into the water above me until he squealed with delight. "Now, my king, we find some peace."

ABOUT THE AUTHOR

M E Rhines is a southwest Florida native currently living in North Port with her two beautiful children and a third, much larger child whom she affectionately calls husband.

She writes young adult paranormal romance to feed her belief that fairy tales are real and nonsense is necessary.

You can also find her adult romances under her edgier alter-ego, Mary Bernsen.

ACKNOWLEDGEMENTS

First and foremost, I have to thank the entire team at Clean Teen Publishing. They have invested just as much time and effort into this series as I have, and I'm eternally grateful for their support. From my amazing cover designer, to the editors and proofreaders, and of course the gals behind the scenes, you're magnificent!

Thank you to my husband and kids for tolerating my obsession with mermaids and allowing me to spend so much time immersed in my imaginary worlds... and to the rest of my family for letting me babble on about them.

And of course, I owe so much to all of my supportive readers. I couldn't keep doing this without you and all your kind words and encouragement.

CPSIA information can be obtained
at www.ICGtesting.com
Printed in the USA
LVHW092211080219
606968LV00001B/1/P

9 781634 223140